THE FUGITIVE FROM
NUREMBERG

THE FUGITIVE FROM
NUREMBERG

FIRMIN G. MAERTENS

*Translated from French to English
by Vivian Maertens Langohr*

DORRANCE
PUBLISHING CO
EST. 1920
PITTSBURGH, PENNSYLVANIA 15238

Dorrance Publishing Co
585 Alpha Drive
Pittsburgh, PA 15238
Visit our website at *www.dorrancebookstore.com*

ISBN: 978-1-6480-4947-7
eISBN: 978-1-6480-4544-8

I dedicate this book to my father's grandchildren and great grandchildren, with special mention to his grandson, Troy Maertens, who was not able to read the book before I finished translating it, due to his untimely death at the age of 44.

Vivian Maertens Langohr

CHAPTER ONE

1939, Hitler rolls over Poland. England and France, after acquiescing for years, allowing the German war machine to threaten other countries, has finally declared war on Germany. Belgium is invaded, overrun, and surrenders within eighteen days. Belgian soldiers attempting to return home are quickly rounded up and herded onto trains and shipped to POW camps in Germany.

Escape!!! The thought haunted Jean Stassard's every waking moment. In his heart, he felt that perhaps, he, more than any of the others, who shared his dismal fate, was the most demoralized of all the men at the prisoner of war camp in Nuremberg. He was consumed by an endless feeling of nostalgia and the gloom of despair had invaded his soul, embittering him to the very core of his existence. He regressed into a dull silence and rejected any attempt at friendship, to allow himself to be alone to wallow in dreams of his country and his own. His own! They were few and he loved them dearly.

First, there was his mother. When the mobilization began, she suffered a great deal from being separated from her only child, but she would still see him on occasion, when he was on leave from the army. Since Belgium's surrender, when he had been captured and forced into this cruel, inhumane place in Nuremberg where the Germans held hundreds of prisoners of war, he had been away for months on end. Jean deeply resented the pain he knew she must be enduring since May 28 of the previous year, not knowing where he was or whether he was even dead or alive.

His father, fifty-five years of age, stooped from all the years of heavy labor, had always been very proud of his son, although, he had always concealed his feelings — as is customary with the simple country folk, who considered it a weakness for a man to show emotion. The man's grief manifested itself in the evening hours when he would sit sadly by the fire, staring blindly into the flickering flames of the fireplace while smoking his pipe.

Mariette, his fiancée, whose love for Jean was very intense but sad, knew he cared for her. Yet she also realized that he did not feel in his heart the extreme joy, the intoxicating happiness she experienced at the slightest touch of his hand. Often, she had asked him if he loved her and he had always answered in the affirmative, although, he had never passionately held her shivering body in his arms and murmured words of love and tenderness. She knew that he would someday grow to love her as he had in her dreams. She would be a suitable wife and there was no reason why they should not have a good life together.

His homeland: Ah, yes, the small village with the old bell tower on the summit of a small hill. How he longed to see it again.

His childhood home was quite a distance from the others in a valley through which a small river traced a winding ribbon to the horizon. The creek ran behind Jean's house where the young man had spent endless hours daydreaming under the tall poplars, while dangling his feet in the cool limpid water.

To his country he attached this multitude of small pleasures; insignificant events that pass by uneventfully and to which we never give a second thought, although these insignificant things totally fill our lives. The evening chats around the fireplace, sitting under a large tree in the summer, as a gentle breeze fans the heat of the day. Reading the current events in the local paper, having a cup of coffee or a pint of beer accompanied by friends. Joking and talking, eating until you can't eat another bite, and going to bed late and sleeping in. All these things are taken for granted. Until they are snatched away!!!

Yet this all seemed so long ago, in another world. The days went by so slowly, as if time were standing still. It was as if decades had passed since he had been forced to leave his village: a paradise lost. At first, he kept the faith that he would be released and returned to Belgium. He had already seen many POWs released without explanation to take the road back home. His liberation date had been posted many times, only to be postponed. Always, hope was replaced with despair, each new date making him yearn for his freedom, again and again as a desperate soul needs to hold on to some hope no matter how small and unattainable or it drives him mad. This situation had attacked him to the very core of his existence, and he had become extremely suspicious of everything and everyone; he believed nothing and trusted no one. Without admitting it, he knew deep down the inevitability, that his captivity would not be terminated until this ugly war ended.

The small bits of news that filtered into the camp had convinced him of the fact that many years would pass before this torment would cease. It seemed that month after month other countries were drawn into this worldwide conflict and one could almost predict who would be next to enter this dreadful war in the months to come.

He had become indifferent to the issues of the war. In the beginning, he had prayed for Germany's defeat. Now, he cared little about who would be the winner. He detested this land of exile with all his being and his thoughts were dominated by the burning desire to be free. Each day, this foreign soil burned more and more under his feet and his sadness and desperation increased. Most of the other inmates who shared his plight, had succumbed to this life in the stalag, but not Jean. He wanted to be emancipated, returned to his country, to his loved ones. And if he wasn't soon granted his freedom, he would take it!

CHAPTER TWO

During his endless nights of insomnia in the barracks of the stalag, he devised a plan of escape. He had gone over every detail, examined all the possibilities, and weighed all the pros and cons of every aspect of his plan. He would need to rely on his geographic recollection of the area in Germany that separated Nuremberg from the Belgian frontier, hundreds of kilometers away. It was a huge distance; he had no idea what was waiting for him along the way, and he was also counting on a little luck. He must be daring, cautious, and alert; he continued to repeat this to himself.

His greatest difficulty would be in getting out of the city of Nuremberg and covering a relatively large distance before the escape was discovered and the German police began to track him down. Week after week, month after month, he had saved the paltry wage paid to POWs for their forced work. Pfennig by pfennig, until now when he felt he had enough funds in his possession to make the voyage without having to rely on the charity of the general population. Begging would take time and could arouse suspicion, dashing all his hopes.

The day he had chosen to execute his plan was extremely cold. It was the month of January and everything was covered in frost. As usual, a truck had transported Jean and other prisoners to the factory where they had been forced to work for weeks. Jean had worn a pair of civilian shoes he still had in his possession and a pair of pants that he had bought from another inmate. He carried his cap, his vest, his hood, and military issue, which were dirty and well worn. This ensemble was nothing exceptional. All his companions had replaced one or another item of their uniform they had once been so proud of, with an alternate that they had procured through buying, swapping, or even by stealing. They tended to resemble a band of bandits rather than soldiers.

In the morning, his first responsibility, was to clean the offices of the stalag and today, as usual, while the workers were entering the complex, he went to the janitor's closet, filled a pail with water, and picked up a mop and returned to set about his tasks. He pushed open the door to the employee's rest room and began to mop the floor. The anticipation of what he was about to do made him shiver even more than the harshness of the weather. After glancing in the mirror over the sink, it pleased him to note that none of the tension and agitation he was feeling showed on his face. After he finished, he moved on to the first office, paused a moment, immobile and thoughtful and entered the room, checking to make sure everything he did looked the same as usual.

He was careful to do his job just as efficiently and neatly as he always did; trying to appear calm, but his heart was racing with a mixture of fear and hope. If, for a moment his hands looked like they were trembling, it should appear to others to be because of the frigid water he was using. Frequently during his duties, he paused to listen for any unusual noise that might reach his ears now and then, but all the sounds he heard were the normal day to day sounds from typewriters, adding machines and the murmur of voices; he could hear nothing out of the ordinary.

He had just finished cleaning the second office when the employees began to enter. As usual, there was the typical greeting from the office workers, which he acknowledged with a smile and as much fake enthusiasm as he had other mornings. In the past several weeks they had grown accustomed to seeing him here. Quite often they would give him a cigarette or a piece of bread. The prisoners of war were treated very well at the stalag - no one would dare dispute it, but they all knew that any one of the prisoners at any time would accept the smallest morsel of food they were given with enthusiasm; even moldy bread.

Meanwhile, he became extremely eager to get this job done; the critical moment was at hand. He began to work more quickly. When his chores were complete, he returned the cleaning equipment to their proper place. As he entered the cloakroom in the hall, he listened intently. He could hear the clicking of a typewriter, and the murmur of people in conversation, but no sound of telltale footsteps reached his ears. Then, instead of putting on the military issue he had worn on his arrival, he grabbed a civilian jacket off the rack. With the same swiftness, he made use of a good brown overcoat and hat, he had noticed on previous days. One would have thought they were made to measure for him, proof of the painstaking care he had taken in planning his escape.

He walked quickly down the hall, out the door, then took a quick glance around the courtyard and reassured that there was no one in sight, with rapid steps, he walked towards the gate that accessed the street and opened it... he was no longer a prisoner, but he was now a fugitive.

CHAPTER THREE

Jean put up the collar of his pilfered overcoat. It had become terribly cold and the sky was covered with gray clouds, announcing the threat of snow, but the fugitive was pleased. The harshness of the weather allowed him to wrap himself up, although he did feel a certain amount of anxiety; fear that a passerby would identify him as a P.O.W. Since no one paid any attention to him, his angst diminished and nearly disappeared at times. With deep breaths, he filled his lungs with emancipated air. A sense of freedom rediscovered: going where you wish, doing what you want, being allowed to move freely on the streets among people. Having shaken the nerve-wracking routine of the stalag, this was so intoxicating he was barely conscious of it.

A little at a time he slowed his gait and began to stroll, looking in store windows; bakeries, butcher shops, bookstores, just trying to look normal. In his pocket, he fingered the German money he had accumulated during his long months in captivity. He didn't dare enter the bakery to buy a loaf of bread even though he had suffered cruelly from hunger for so long.

As he wandered, he decided the first thing he should do, was to leave Nuremberg as quickly as possible. He was not familiar with the city; the only road he had traveled was the one that led from the P.O.W. camp to the factory where he had worked. To find his way to the train station, he would be forced to ask for directions. His knowledge of the German language was pretty good, but there was a possibility that his accent could give him away. He needed to be prudent and as brief as possible with his inquiries. At the corner of a street, he read the name *Tucherstrasse*. This meant nothing to him, nor did the names *Bismarkstrasse* or *Schillerstrasse*. He hesitated, trying to decide in which direction to go, and noticed an old man walking with small steps on the other side of the street. He decided to question the man because elderly people are inclined to talk a lot and are always ready to volunteer information.

He crossed the street and as he pressed on to catch up with the old man, he passed three women in deep conversation. Suddenly, he was shocked to hear the word *Kriegsgefangene* (P.O.W.) uttered by one of them. He continued, without daring to look back; he could feel his heart beating in his throat. A few steps further, he became unsure that he had understood correctly, yet he dared not change his pace; on the contrary, he had to work hard not to give in to the urge to run. He was imagining that all passersby knew that a prisoner of war had escaped, and that all eyes were fixed on him. He reached the old man and as he passed, he merely glanced at him, not daring to address him. The man continued walking, unconcerned, as he puffed on his porcelain pipe.

Jean arrived at Obsmarkt, passed the church of Notre Dame and reached the Adolf Hitler Platz. Not until then, did he venture to turn around. No one was following; everyone passed by without a single look of suspicion. He took a deep breath and approached a woman in her fifties.

-Bahnhof, Fraulein?

The woman showed him Plobenhofstrasse and told him to stay on it to the end, and then take Konigstrasse; the train station would be at the end of the street.

The fugitive muttered a thank you and took the route indicated. Plobenhofstrasse was quite short and soon Jean arrived at the Peignitz, the river that divided the old city of Nuremberg into two sections. He passed the Museumbruck and turned onto Konigstrasse. Despite the frigid weather, there seemed to be a spirited air about the crowds on this street, giving him a comforting sense of security. His heart beat faster as he approached the station hoping that this was not where he would gamble away his fate: the failure or success of his escape.

He slowed his step, as he wanted to prolong the time he had wished for yet dreading it as well. He paused for an instant to admire the tower of the Sankt-Lorenz Kirche and the rose window above the portal door, but then, realizing that this act could make him stand out as a stranger in the city, he pushed on.

I must do nothing to arouse any suspicion, he reminded himself. *I can't be too careful.*

Shortly, he found himself across from a huge tower: the Frauentor. On the other side of the street was the train station. He crossed Bahnofplatz and casually passed through the door marked *"Eingang"* (entrance).

First, his eyes swept over the crowd that filled the waiting room. There were many men in uniforms that were not familiar to him, but the uniforms he recognized, apart from the military uniforms, were those of the local police and his heart again began to race. He didn't have a single piece of I.D.; he had taken great care to destroy all his personal papers in case he found himself in a situation where he would need to disclose his nationality. Better that he would have nothing on him to reveal that he was Belgian. If he should be asked for I.D., there was one chance in a hundred that maybe they would discover his prisoner of war status. Nevertheless, it was absolutely the biggest gamble of his life. He would constantly need to be on guard, in case the police decided to conduct an inspection among the passengers, which could happen at any time. If this should happen, his plan was to leave the station and try to reach another on foot; the Furth Station maybe.

At that moment, he noticed a departure timetable on the wall. As he perused the list of names, two cities caught his eye: Wurzbourg and Mannheim. If he went in either of these directions he would draw nearer to Belgium, that is if his recollection of the geography of this region was correct and he knew it was.

His thoughts drifted once more to his country. Belgium was so far away!!

He uttered a big sigh as he moved toward the ticket counter trying to decide which of the two directions to take. As luck would have it, directly ahead of him was a young woman with two suitcases. She asked for a ticket to Manheim and paid. Jean watched her every move and immediately his decision was made. He used the same words, paid the same amount of money, and hurriedly followed the young passenger. There was no need for inquiries; the only thing he had to do, was to follow the young lady.

Staying a couple of feet behind her, he reached the platform without losing sight of her and picked his way through the throng of people heading in every direction. The young girl certainly knew this station well, he observed; she walked confidently and without hesitation and she ended up picking an empty compartment. The fugitive followed her and sat opposite the girl without daring to make eye contact. His eyes wandered to the waiting room and for what seemed like an eternity, he gazed impassively at the people passing.

He took on an air of indifference although he was burning with impatience, awaiting only the train's departure. The clock on the right said 10:30. He glanced at the clock again and he remembered a similar clock with a pendulum at his parent's home. Then, all the nostalgia that had accumulated in his soul for all these months came back in a rush of emotion and hope mixed with anxiety, making him shiver nervously.

Finally, Jean Stassart risked a discreet glance at the young woman sitting across from him. She seemed to be lost in thought and he took the opportunity to observe her with a little more detail. She was very pretty, and he guessed that she wasn't quite twenty. She had large sad brown eyes, a good figure, and beautiful red hair. She was of small build and tastefully dressed. She did not seem to represent the typical strong, robust German woman who dominated Germany at this time.

Sensing the young man's eyes on her, she returned his stare and their eyes met. He began to feel uncomfortably embarrassed and he was glad that at that moment other passengers were beginning to fill the compartment. A middle-aged man and woman took their place next to him. The man immediately started chatting with his companion about current events. He discussed the situation at the Grecian-Italian front and in Albania, reinforcing his comments by showing her an article in the local newspaper, *"Acht-Uren Blatt"* which he held out for her to see. The couple ignored all the other passengers on board.

For a moment Jean had forgotten that there were still battles and conflicts going on at so many points around the globe. The prisoners at the stalag in Nuremberg had rejoiced at the news of the setbacks suffered by the Italians in Greece and Albania. Despite the conditions at the stalag, some news, even news that was unfavorable to the Germans or their allies, managed to spread through the camp like wild fire and everyone, even though they were captives, knew what was happening on the world stage regarding this dreadful war.

The fugitive became increasingly nervous and with each passing minute, his impatience grew. Was this train ever going to get on the way?

In his agitated state, he shuffled his feet, and by accident, he nudged the girl's feet sitting across from him.

"Pardon," he said.

Without thinking, he had blurted out a word in French and he realized he had made his first mistake. His nerves had played a dirty trick on him. Hopefully, the young German hadn't noticed! He looked at her in desperation, but the shock he read in her eyes left him no doubt; she had understood and understood well. Seeing the young man's predicament, she could not help but stifle a smile.

"You didn't hurt me," she said.

He answered in German:

"Please understand that it was my fault, mada… …."

He had nearly said the word "mademoiselle" it was obvious that he was not in control. He held on to the feeble hope that this time she hadn't noticed, but if she did, she would be certain that this young man was a foreigner. He began to regret having followed her.

The wretched expression on his face made her laugh again. He returned the smile, but he was furious with himself for having let down his guard. To appear nonchalant, he looked out the window at the gray sky and said in a light tone:

"I… … …I think it's going to snow."

The young girl burst out laughing, which made the fugitive even more uncomfortable. He wondered what she thought was so funny. The statement he had made was very commonplace; he didn't find it at all funny.

"You seem very tense;" She remarked in a light mocking tone with a mischievous look in her eyes.

"No, of course not," he protested. "You could even say that I'm perfectly at ease."

She continued to laugh silently.

"It seems to me you're not relaxed at all. Perhaps my presence makes you uncomfortable."

She continued to tease him, but there was also a certain kindness in her voice, which warmed his heart. It had been so long since anyone had addressed him in this fashion. All this time he had heard only orders, harsh words, and indifference.

"Oh! No! I assure you. Your presence doesn't bother me in the least!" He objected.

"Are you always so uneasy when you're with a girl?" she continued jokingly, much to his irritation.

He was hoping that keeping up a conversation with his fellow commuter would help him achieve his goal and he fully intended to keep her talking until they arrived at their destination. Little by little, his edginess subsided, and he began to feel as if he was in control of the situation again. He smiled and answered:

"No, I believe that this is the first time I've found myself flustered in the presence of a young lady, but I haven't found myself in the company of a girl like you for quite some time."

"What makes me so different?" she said.

Jean thought to himself that her looks and her smile were the most beautiful he had ever seen in his life.

"One isn't always lucky enough to see such beautiful eyes," he said.

He observed with pleasure that his statement did not faze her, although her face took on a pink flush. She averted her eyes and answered:

"Men! If in an hour you should be sitting across from another woman you would probably tell her the same thing."

"Don't think that. It has been almost thirty years that I've been noticing women and I honestly admit that I've never met anyone quite like you."

"But you don't know me."

"Unfortunately, no."

The train started up and Jean let out a sigh of relief, oblivious to the beauty in front of him or the crowd outside as they exited the station. He noticed several policemen and a few other men in uniform making hand signals and stopping passengers to ask for I.D. papers. Were they searching for the escaped prisoner of war? No, impossible; the missing clothes could not have been discovered yet. The employees would not find them missing until at least noon; about an hour from now, when they would only notice the robbery. The missing prisoner who worked in the factory would only be missed in the evening, at roll call, when they returned to the camp. His companions would realize he was missing, but they wouldn't be surprised. Quite often one prisoner or another would alienate himself to make plans of escape, and even if the others suspected one of their fellow inmates was planning an escape, none of them would reveal his intent.

After some reflection, the prisoner concluded that the search conducted by the police at the Nuremberg station was not aimed toward him. He became more and more at ease and felt a great relief to be putting some distance between himself and this city where he had spent the worst period of his entire life.

CHAPTER FOUR

A light fog hung in the air, and as the last of the houses faded into the distance, the train traveled at full speed through the countryside, wrapped in its winter sleep. Jean again addressed the young German.

"Do you always travel alone?

"In fact, I travel very little," she answered, "but this time I am undertaking the biggest journey of my life."

"You consider the trip from Nuremberg to Mannheim that great a voyage? And you have never traveled further than that?"

"I'm going much further than Mannheim, but why do you think that I'm going to Manheim?"

"You were ahead of me at the ticket counter when you bought your ticket. I seem to remember you saying 'Mannheim.'"

She laughed again showing her perfectly straight white teeth.

"Oh! Then you are following me?"

"Following is not the right word. I assure you that I had no intention…"

"What were your intentions then?" She interrupted, with a mischievous voice.

He laughed in turn, appreciative of the young traveler's sense of humor.

"You… … …you," he began; but he could not find the words to express his thoughts.

"Me?" She asked innocently.

"You are charming!"

"You don't know me and you're paying me all these compliments. Don't be fooled by appearances; I am insufferable. My friends would agree unanimously."

"Permit me to say that I don't share their opinion and I find it a real pleasure listening to you talk."

The train slowed down, passed a small station, but didn't stop. Jean read the name of locality: Heilsbronn. The trip continued through a sandy, gritty plain; here and there he noticed pine forests, but the countryside was sparsely inhabited. The fugitive thought if he had to undertake this trip for one reason or another, the rare inhabitants would have regarded him with distrust and would long remember a stranger had passed through the area.

"And you," inquired the young female, "are you going to Mannheim?"

"Yes," he said, avoiding her eyes.

"You can't be from Nuremberg or Mannheim; you don't speak in a dialect from either place," she remarked.

"As a matter of fact," he said hesitantly, "I'm from Aix-la-Chapelle (Aachen)."

He blurted out the name of this city knowing that it was situated near the Belgian border and it was possible that his accent was more typical of that region. *If necessary, it could also explain his habit of speaking in the French tongue,* he thought.

"Well then," she continued, "you have visited Nuremberg? You're going to Mannheim and you live in Aix-la-Chapelle? Do you travel frequently."

"Frequently, that's not the word," answered Jean. "I have an uncle who lives in Nuremberg whom I visited, and I have a married sister who lives in Mannheim. I'm taking the opportunity to spend a few days with her."

As he said all this, he shifted his eyes because he could feel himself blushing. He was ashamed that he was forced to lie to her this way, and he was surprised how easily he had told her these lies.

"What a coincidence," she explained. "I am nearly in the same situation as you are. The only difference is that I'm going to spend a day with my sister-in-law who lives in Mannheim. Her husband, my brother, is a soldier and he's serving with the occupation forces in Belgium at this moment."

For an instant, her face took on a pensive look and she appeared to be a little sad, and he felt as if he was seeing her eyes for the first time. She continued:

"You seem to have a lot of leisure time. Have you never been a soldier?" Regardless of all the pleasure he had talking to her, Jean began to regret ever having started. The conversation seemed to have turned into an interrogation, unintentionally, of course; nevertheless, she was becoming too curious. He had begun to lie, and he feared having to continue, as well as having to be prudent and consider each word before he spoke it. After all, he didn't know the young person sitting across from him, and if she discovered anything incriminating or even had any suspicions, he didn't know how she would react. She could alert the authorities at one or the other stations the train pulled into. He resolved to double his awareness and if the situation became dangerous, he would disappear.

He glanced at the couple occupying the other part of the compartment and was relieved to see that they were engrossed in their conversation and not paying any attention to them.

"I am a soldier," said the escapee, "but I'm on vacation at this moment."

"And you travel without wearing your uniform?"

He could read the astonishment on his interrogator's face and he was vaguely aware that he had just made another mistake. The young German's eyes seemed to penetrate his as she leaned towards him, so closely that their hands touched.

"But do you know what a big chance you're taking?" She whispered.

"Certainly," he answered indifferently and a little boastfully. "I've been wearing my uniform for so long I couldn't resist the urge to be like everyone else for a change. You can't imagine how good it feels. I don't need to be saluting or standing when a superior enters a room. I feel more at ease, more liberated."

"This liberty could be very costly." She said.

"Oh! I'm not worried," he answered nonchalantly.

"But suppose the exit at Mannheim is controlled, how would you avoid detection?"

"I would say I'm a businessman," he said, trying to sound as calm as possible.

A distressing anxiety began to clutch at his heart. As a matter of fact, what would he do if the police were to check the papers of those exiting the station at Mannheim? Meanwhile, with a small smile on his lips and as naturally as possible, he added:

"Anyhow, you wouldn't betray me, would you?"

He found it difficult to read her expression, but he felt deep relief when she answered in a soft voice:

"No, I wouldn't betray you."

Spontaneously, he seized the girl's hands.

"I'm very grateful," he said. "I thank you with all my heart. But enough talk about me, let's talk about you for a while. First, is it too much to ask you your name?"

"Hilda Hessling."

"What a lovely name!"

"That's a trite compliment. People always say that."

"But it's true and I don't say that to everyone," he assured her. "Permit me to introduce myself: Heinrich Lutz."

"What a lovely name!"

They both burst out laughing. The atmosphere had suddenly changed; they no longer felt like strangers. Something had touched him, and Jean was fearful that when it came time to part, he would regret it.

"I seem to remember that you are going to Mannheim to see your sister-in-law, and that this is the biggest trip of your life."

He had previously asked her the same thing, but she had evaded his question. He repeated it now because he wanted to know where she was going after this visit.

Without admitting it, he hoped to be able to continue his trip with her after Mannheim.

"Then," she answered, "Remember too, that I'm only spending the day with her, not even a full day. Tomorrow I'll continue on my way."

"Mannheim, then is not the end of your trip? At the risk of being insensitive, may I ask where you're traveling afterwards."

"You are very inquisitive. I'm going to Belgium."

"To Belgium!" He exclaimed stupefied.

"You say 'to Belgium' with a pleasant smile," she said. "Does this surprise you?"

"My God, I'm astonished! With this war going on and the Belgians under German occupation, why in the world are you heading to Belgium? It seems to me to be very dangerous."

"I'm going to see my brother."

Jean tried to put some order in his chaotic thoughts attempting to sort things out. What luck! such possibilities! Such dangers! What a coincidence that Hilda Hessling was taking the same trip he was. In his mind, he was already making plans to remain in her company for the rest of the trip to Belgium. His safety could depend on it.

"And your sister-in-law, your brother's wife, is she accompanying you?" He questioned.

He waited anxiously for her reply, because if she answered in the affirmative, it could greatly complicate things.

"No," declared Hilda, "she will not accompany me. She can't leave her baby. My brother has never seen his daughter and I will take him some photographs. He'll be very happy!"

"And you undertake this long voyage in mid-winter and alone just to see your brother? You must love him a lot and you're very courageous."

"Yes," she said dreamily, "I love him very much. He is three years older than I am and we've always been such good friends. My parents had no objections when I told them of my intention to go to Belgium. It's been a year since we've seen him."

"How will you locate him? I must say you'll have a great deal of difficulty in finding him considering the state of the war. Do you realize that now and then soldiers change their quarters? Finding a soldier in a strange country in time of war is probably as difficult as finding a needle in a haystack."

"It won't be as difficult as all that." She said, "A few weeks ago, one of his buddies came to Nuremberg on leave and told us that my brother was in Antwerp. His friend gave me the address of a hotel there and I'll wait until my brother contacts me. If he's no longer in Antwerp, he will find me there wherever he is."

She was quiet and remained pensive for a moment, while he devoured her eyes, finding her more and more charming. Then, the memory of another young girl assailed him, his Marriette, who was awaiting his return in his small village. A great sadness overtook him. He could not pinpoint the cause of his sorrow, but she was there, real and painful, in his conscience.

"I regret that we can't travel together up to Aix-la-Chapelle," said Hilda again. "Since you'll be spending several days in Mannheim and I'm leaving there tomorrow…"

She didn't continue her sentence, but turned towards the fugitive and resumed:

"It's not very pleasant for a girl to travel so far alone."

"Actually," he said smiling, "I presume the way you're talking that my company would not be unpleasant."

"No, not too much," she answered, teasing.

"But I'm still just a stranger to you."

"Not really. I know your name and you have confided in me. I am convinced that you are an honest man."

He didn't answer; each word she uttered renewed in him new feelings, and he didn't know what approach to take. At the same time, he wondered if he could figure out a pretext to continue the trip with her after Mannheim. He could admit the truth later, if the time would come to confess.

The locomotive slowed its pace, the brakes grinding, and the train stopped at Ansbach Station.

CHAPTER FIVE

The anxiety over the success of his escape had dissipated slightly; for the time being; he didn't foresee any immediate danger. However, another concern began to gnaw at him. Other than the small crust of bread he had eaten that morning, before he reported for work, he had taken no nourishment during the previous few hours. It was certain that until his arrival in Mannheim, it would have been impossible to try to procure something to eat. He wasn't even sure how to go about finding something once he arrived in the city. He hadn't thought about the possibility of the rationing going on in Germany, but he did vaguely remember overhearing conversations about it although there were constant changes in regulations. He had money, but that might not be enough, he might need a ration card.

Also, it could be several days until he reached the Belgian border and the idea of not having anything to eat made him shudder. He had learned to know starvation at the camp and the thought of the pain it left in his stomach frightened him.

As he pondered his current situation, the future looked very grim, yet, his thoughts always came back to the young girl seated across from him. His trust in her grew with each moment and he was convinced that he would have his next meal with her help, and that the success of his mission would depend largely on her as well.

"Ansbach is a lovely city, is it not?" she remarked.

Jean glanced at the rooves and frontages of the buildings. The sky was still dark, and a few snowflakes began to fall lightly and silently on the ground.

"I have never visited this city," he said.

"My aunt lives in Ansbach and I've been here several times," explained the young girl. "She's very proud of her city and she claims that the castle is much more beautiful and important than the one in Wurzbourg. Have you ever been to the castle of Wurzbourg?"

"No."

"My aunt told me a story of Kasper Hauser," continued Hilda. "He was found dead as an infant and his death as well as his birth has always remained a mystery. I never had much faith in my aunt's stories, since she has quite a vivid imagination, but there is certainly a basis for the one about Kasper Hauser. In the Hofgarten there is a commemorative stone in his memory. There are many beautiful forests around Ansbach, and I love going for walks here."

The train started back up and soon the city of Ansbach disappeared over the horizon.

"It seems as if you love nature, trips, and tales," said Jean.

"Yes, I love all of these things, but I have yet to realize my biggest dream, which is to see the sea."

"You've never seen the sea?" exclaimed Jean. "I've been there dozens of times, to Ostende to Blankenberghe, to…"

He stopped short and looked at his interrogator with dread; once more he had forgotten his situation and blurted out the names of some Belgian cites hastily. Her next sentence left him with no doubt that she had caught on to what he was saying.

"But Ostende is a Belgian city. Have you been to Belgium?"

"Yes. I've been there several times. I am stationed in Belgium, right now, in Brugge, not far from the coast."

"When do you go back?"

"In two to three days, immediately after my departure from Manheim."

He looked sadly at the scenery as it passed swiftly by the train: "That is if everything goes as planned," he said to himself.

The terrain was becoming more and more hilly, and the snowflakes were falling thicker and heavier. Suddenly, Jean was taken back to his own village where he had had such a wonderful life; he mused. The little houses with red roofs, the old church tower, and his country home, would never again mean the same thing to him as they did in the past. This pleasant scene, this happy atmosphere, would be lacking something: Hilda Hessling would not be there. Hilda Hessling! The name rang out to him like a musical note, seductive and distant, which left an undefinable sadness deep in his heart.

His eyes fell on the pretty face of the young girl and it swathed him with admiration and with some bitterness. Tonight, he would leave her and never see her again! Never again! Amid all the uncertainties that surrounded him, this was inevitable, he thought with sorrow. In these last few hours, he had become so enamored with this girl. He had never felt like this about anyone. In his wildest dreams he had never imagined that he would have these kinds of feelings, let alone for a German woman. No, it wasn't possible! He refused to believe he would never see her again; it would be like leaving a part of himself... and her absence would leave a deep void in his life.

Hilda was lost in her own daydreams. What was she thinking? He would have given anything to know. After he leaves her, she will occupy all his thoughts and the prospect of separating was already causing him a lot of sorrow. He would have done anything in his power to avoid leaving this young girl he had only known for a few hours. However, he realized that he had a certain satisfaction in knowing that hopefully, she was feeling the same way and she would possibly also suffer a little when he left.

Presently, the train stopped at another station: Crailsheim. Nearby, stood a church whose clock said 3:00. A thin layer of snow began to cover the rooves of the buildings of this city.

It was again Hilda who broke the silence.

"The sea, is it as beautiful as they say?"

"Yes. I've always loved the sea," said Jean. I've often spent hours sitting on the sand gazing at her. I used to shade my eyes and follow the clouds projected on the sparkling surface of the water and I loved it when the sun disappeared in the billowing waves on a warm summer night. Sometimes, I would watch the waves wash into shore and sit on the beach as I wondered what mysterious force could move this immense sheet of water without ever ceasing. I think that the most wonderful thing in the world would be to sit on the shore by the sea, seated next to the one you love.

"Have you ever been in love?" She asked gently.

"No... ... never."

He fell silent. The landscape they were traveling through after Crailsheim was quite mountainous and Jean compared it to the Belgian Ardennes. The view was a little obscure because of the dull light and the never ceasing snowfall, and soon it would be evening.

A village was visible through the hazy curtain of snow; it was situated at the foot of a mountain whose peak disappeared into the low clouds.

"Hessenthal," announced the young girl; "the hill you see over there is Einkorn; it's 510 meters high."

"You know the country very well," observed the fugitive.

"It's my country and I love it very much. It's too bad that it's so gloomy today; you would have had a chance to enjoy all the beauty of this area. You've never been here in the summer?"

"No. Never, I've only been in Nuremberg once. It was in the summer, but it wasn't the way we're going now; it was by way of Wurzbourg and Furth."

The Einkorn had disappeared behind the dark horizon. A few minutes later, the train stopped at another station: Hall. This small village, situated in a deep valley, extended gradually to the left bank of the Kocher, a tributary of the Neckar. The snow had stopped falling and the clouds were not as thick. Here and there a small amount of blue sky peeked through, and even though night was approaching, it was beginning to clear up a little. The trip continued in a westerly direction.

Jean admired the series of high mountains and the old villages and, here and there, the ruins of an old castle, built centuries ago. Hilda knew quite a few of them and called them by name. She even told about their history. First, there was Neuenstein, a beautiful castle of the 15th or 16th century; then Oeringen, a castle built in the 10th century with its flamboyant collegiate style. Finally, the young German recognized Weinberg and the castle of Weibertreu, the subject of the famous legend of Weibertreu, which rose to a height of 265 meters.

The fugitive had, in his young companion, a perfect guide, and if it wasn't for the hunger and his present circumstances, he may have found this trip the most enjoyable he had ever taken.

Meanwhile, night was coming swiftly now and by the time the train stopped again at another station, which Hilda identified as Heilbronn, the darkness was almost complete. The lights cast a soft bluish hue on the ground, while outside the station, the brightness of the snow made it easy to distinguish objects at a distance.

Seeing some movement on the platform drew the prisoner's attention to the presence of several men in uniform that seemed to be awaiting the train's arrival. Some of the passengers presented themselves at the exits and as they left the railway cars, they were stopped and required to show their identification.

At that moment, Jean's heart skipped a beat. No doubt they were searching for someone. Further down, he noticed some policemen boarding the car coming from Nuremberg. It must be him they were looking for.

His mind worked quickly; he needed to make plans with extraordinary speed. His breathing was very rapid. His eyes searched in all directions, like an animal sensing danger. He could tell that the young woman was also looking at the scene, which was unfolding on the platform with curiosity, but if she had any suspicions about his predicament, she didn't let on, which made him feel a little more comfortable.

"Excuse me," he said.

Before she had a chance to say anything, he left the compartment and moved to the other end of the car where he found a bathroom. He hurriedly entered, being sure that no one was paying any attention to him. He was so scared; his legs were feeling shaky and he had to find something to hang onto for fear he might fall. He remained in this position for several moments and brought his hand up to his heart feeling the heavy beating. As he did this, his fingers moved over an object which he felt in the inside pocket of his overcoat. He was very still for a moment, incapable of making the slightest movement. Then, slowly, he slid his right hand into the pocket and retrieved a billfold. He opened it, but in the poor light he could not determine the amount of cash in it, yet he was convinced that it looked like a great sum of money.

He felt as if the earth was giving way under his feet and his head dropped to his chest like an accused prisoner being sentenced to death. He no longer had any doubt that it was surely he they were looking for: prisoner of war, escapee, and thief. He would never be able to convince these men who would confront him that he was unaware of how this wallet had found itself in his overcoat. He was searching his brain trying to understand. Perhaps the owner of this coat had forgotten that he had put the money in his pocket. Wait, it was payday at the factory; perhaps this money was the worker's salary. Could one possibly be so distracted that he would leave such a large amount of money in his pocket without fearing that it might be stolen? He was sure of one thing; he had this money in his hands, and it could be the cause of his escape being discovered more quickly than he thought it might have been. His pursuers surely would want this payroll back as soon as possible. A combination of circumstances had put him at the forefront of a situation he could not have foreseen, and he couldn't wrap his head around the fact that he had just discovered this terrible mistake he had made and hoping he had not made any other unforeseen slip-ups. He felt his reason begin to weaken in a rush of crazy thoughts. He imagined large posters with his name in big print offering a large reward to the person having information leading to his capture. He could see guns drawn on him; all the policemen of the Reich in pursuit and last, even Hilda Hessling denouncing him with words of scorn and hatred. He chastised himself for not having taken more precaution, due to being so consumed by his own personal misery.

As he sat wondering what to do next, little by little, he began to look at his situation more calmly. First, he needed to rid himself of the incriminating billfold and its contents. Throwing it away at this point was too dangerous; it would leave too much of a trail and could cause the police to search everyone on the train. He must remain hidden until the train leaves the station and hope that nobody would be looking for him here. Afterwards, if he crossed a deserted or uninhabited area, he could perhaps throw the evidence of the theft out the window. Soon, his thoughts went to the young German, like a ship-wrecked person on a faraway island. He remembered the words she had uttered.

"I will not betray you."

She had said this concerning him not wearing his uniform and the danger it could cause him travelling in civilian clothes. Her tone reassured him, and he felt he could trust her, although, his case now was much more serious than being out of uniform. It would all depend on what point of view she would take of this situation. It was possible that, once she learned of his deception and discovered the identity of her travelling companion, she might consider him a traitor to her country. He had heard of the spirit of patriotism, and exaggerated fanaticism of the single party system in Germany. Those who accepted the doctrines of the Nazi party were like a cult or a religion. He didn't know, however, if Hilda Hessling belonged to this group. But his confidence in her wasn't shaken, deep down, he sensed that she wouldn't betray him.

CHAPTER SIX

He was very vigilant; constantly listening for outside noises, but the sounds were unclear, and he learned nothing. He would have given anything to see what was happening on the platform and in the cars, but he dared not open the window to check. He waited, and each passing minute for him was a long, tormented eternity. If only the train would start up! In the other train stations (Ansbach, Crailsheim, and Hall) the wait was only two or three minutes; here, the wait had been 15 minutes already. Could it be because this station was more significant, or could it be because they were searching for someone?

Finally, the noise of steel impacting steel along the whole row of cars and a few shocks and tremors, and the train began to move. Jean uttered a sigh of immense relief; he was no longer concerned for the moment. The passengers must all have had their papers inspected and he felt he was in the clear. They would have found whatever they were searching for or they would realize that the suspect was not on the train. His confidence was increasing considerably.

He listened again for a few minutes, and then left his hiding place. First, he looked down the corridor along the compartments, and then carefully began to walk down the aisle, but none of the passengers seemed to pay any attention to him. Reassured, he nonchalantly returned to the compartment he had occupied before the stop in the Heilbronn Station. It seemed extremely quiet and the window curtains had been drawn. The light from the lamps gave everything an eerie glow. Hilda looked surprised when again he took his seat across from her.

"I thought we had parted company," she said.

"Really?" he answered. "Did you think that I would leave without a word of farewell, after we've become such good friends?"

He looked at her reproachfully and half annoyed.

"Do you take me for a man who has no manners, mademoiselle Hessling?"

"How would I know, I've just met you and I barely know you," she said in her defense.

The escapee's face darkened a little.

"When I leave you, it will probably be in a manner that you'll remember for a long time," he said mysteriously.

She seemed not to have heard anything he said, and she asked:

"Did anyone ask you for your papers?"

"No, they didn't, he answered. "If I had been wearing my uniform, I would have been questioned. This way, I look like an ordinary citizen."

"How is it you weren't noticed? They entered the train, and everyone had to show their I.D."

"I was hiding... and you, did you have to show your I.D.?"

"No, because I am a female."

"In fact, it looks to me like all the women were escaping this process. I wonder if maybe it's because the object of this search is a man." She hesitated for a moment and when he looked puzzled, she said,

"Don't you know?"

"Don't I know what?" He asked candidly.

"I guess it's a simple assumption, since everyone is aware of it," she answered dryly.

He bit his lip, then again smiling, he replied, "Then consequently, it wouldn't be difficult for you to tell me this big secret everyone knows about."

"You really don't know? You must be very distracted, or you've been very secluded. Everyone is talking about it."

"I'm not in the habit of eavesdropping; you never get the whole story when you snoop."

He was convinced that she had already guessed he was a very curious sort and she was teasing him, holding back from telling him the information he wanted to know so badly. He decided not to speak about it again, as if he really wasn't interested; just then, she replied:

"If I told you that they're searching for a prisoner of war who escaped from Nuremburg this morning, would you also say that you don't listen to rumors?" His face remained stoic; he tried not to show any expression that would give away his fear. It was hard for him to think that his escape had been discovered after a couple of hours. In a normal tone, he replied:

"No, not at all, if you're the one who told me."

She leaned over, lowering her voice.

"I know something else on the subject of the escapee. Among these policemen, there was a man, my sister-in-law's neighbor."

"And?" he asked, holding his breath.

"He told me the prisoner in question has fled with a considerable sum of money. I even know the individual's description. He stole some clothes he needed and left his in their place."

"What about his description?" asked Jean, beginning to perspire.

"Here it is: 1 meter 65; 30 years old; brown overcoat and a brown hat."

Everything around him began to spin and he became very shaky. The young woman must surely recognize him as the fugitive, and she must be playing a cat and mouse game with him. He felt anger building within him, but he brought it under control. With great difficulty, he calmly uttered these words: "This description seems clear enough."

With some relief, he heard the young woman's words. "I don't find these details all that clear; there are hundreds of people who fit that description. For instance," Hilda started snickering, "You meet that description exactly. You must be around 30 years old, 1 meter 65, and the clothes you're wearing fit the exact description of the clothes the man they are searching for is wearing. I'm surprised that you haven't already been stopped as the escaped prisoner of war. Granted, you were hiding. It has been exciting: You, getting stopped and accused of being the escaped POW! Don't you find that thrilling in a way?" she said, with a good-natured grin.

"Of course; and you, do you find it amusing? Don't forget, that for me, it's been quite annoying given the fact that I'm travelling in civilian clothes." Thinking to himself… *it's human nature that one finds humor in the embarrassment of his fellow man….* Then, trying to change the subject, he asked:

"So, are you leaving Mannheim tomorrow?" "Yes." She said.

He was looking for a pretext to continue the voyage with the young German and he was thinking, without her he would never make his way back to Belgium. But there was also something else… the idea that soon he would have to leave her company forever, was unbearable. He wanted to try to find a way to delay it as much as possible.

"Maybe I'll leave for Aix-la-Chapelle tomorrow," he said. "Then, if you like, we could see each other again tomorrow. Which train are you leaving on?"

"I don't know. I'm not sure of the train schedule going in that direction."

"Would it be possible for us to meet tomorrow morning and we can figure it out?" he asked.

"So, it's a rendezvous you're asking for?" she said with a mischievous twinkle in her eye.

"You don't want to?" said.

"I didn't say that; I would gladly meet you tomorrow morning, but where and at what time?"

"You decide on the time and the place," he said.

"Well if it's convenient for you, how about if I'm at the Hindenburg Bridge at 9:00 tomorrow morning?" She said. "Is that too far from you sister's house? Where does she live, by the way?" In his entire life, he had never been in the city of Mannheim and he didn't know any of the street names. He searched his brain in desperation to come up with an answer to the last question he was asked by the young lady. At the same instant, he remembered that the city was situated on the bank of the Rhine and he said:

"On the Rheinstrasse."

He looked at her an anxiously and waited. Did this street exist, he thought?

"The Rheinstraase," she repeated, "I don't recognize the name. I know the Rheinhausterstrasse and the Rheindeammstrasse. I must say I don't know the city entirely, but yes," she corrected herself and continued to think, "there is a Rheinstrasse, but it's not in Mannhein. It's on the left bank of the Rhine, in Ludwigshafen."

"Indeed, that's right," cried Jean with joy. "It's in Ludwigshafen that I need to go to visit my sister, but she has always maintained that she lives in Mannheim because it's more well-known and Ludwigshafen is more of a suburb of Manheim, so, I too, have been in the habit of saying Mannheim instead of Ludwigshafen."

"And I suppose your sister also thinks it's more important to live in a large city?"

"Women are so arrogant," he said.

"Thank you." she said. "I suppose you recognize Mannheim and you know where the Hindenburg Bridge is."

"I've only been to Ludwigshafen and to Mannheim once or twice and I know very few places, but I should be able to find our place of rendezvous."

"The bridge is on the Neckar and not far from my brother's place; he lives on Neckarstrasse."

"Then it's settled," concluded Jean. "We meet tomorrow morning at 9:00 at the Hindenburg Bridge."

He felt some remorse for having deceived this young woman, who was so self-confident. He wondered silently why she had consented to see him the next day, but in the next instant, he hoped that maybe it was because she might be attracted to him.

"I am dying of hunger," said Hilda as she stood to retrieve her luggage.

Jean jumped up to grab her suitcase before she had a chance to reach it.

In doing so, he nudged her involuntarily and she clung to him so she wouldn't fall. When he felt her arms go around him, he stopped. Neither one of them uttered a word during this embrace. Their eyes met for an instant, and he sensed that a tender moment had come between them. She pulled away, blushing slightly, and he took her bag.

"Here you are, Mademoiselle," he said, his voice still slightly trembling from the emotion he had just felt.

She silently retrieved a few slices of buttered bread. The prisoner again felt deep down in the pit of his stomach the tiresome torment of hunger. She passed him a slice of bread without raising her eyes and said:

"I notice that you aren't carrying any bags, so you must not have any food. Please accept this and don't worry, you won't be depriving me of any food, I assure you."

"But, I'm not hungry," he argued. "I'm never very hungry during a trip. My uncle even tried to give me some food for my trip, but I didn't accept."

"Really," she said. She had raised her eyes to him and observed that he had fixed his starving eyes on the bread thinking that she hadn't noticed.

She put the bread on the prisoner's lap.

"I hate eating alone," she said, "so do me the pleasure of eating with me or it will put me in a bad mood."

He again hesitated.

"Just to make you happy," he finally agreed.

The young girl wasn't surprised that he ate the sandwich with a voracious appetite; she offered him another piece of bread but despite the hunger pangs coming from deep in his stomach, he refused. He tried as much as possible to erase from his brain, the image of this young person who was continuing to eat.

However, another image crossed his mind. Where would he spend the night in Manheim? Without having one piece of identification on him, it would be impossible for him to rent a hotel room. The thought of spending the night under these beautiful stars in this terrible cold on an empty stomach made him shudder, but he may not have any choice.

CHAPTER SEVEN

The train stopped at yet another station: Heidelberg. Jean knew nothing about the city. When he parted the curtains on the window in front of his compartment, the murky darkness allowed him to see only a few lights passing by in a circle.

After he said that he had never visited this ancient capital of the Palatinat, Hilda explained to him that the University of Heidelberg had been founded here in the 14th century and numbered 14,000 students. The library had around 600,000 volumes and approximately 4,000 manuscripts. The young traveler had visited the cellars of the castle where she had seen the "Grosses Fass," the famous gigantic wine vat of Heidelberg containing over 2,200 hectoliters (100 liters) of wine. She had climbed the Molkekur and the Koningstuhl, the two high hills found on the left bank of the Neckar. The later one reaching a height of 578 meters.

On the right bank of the Neckar she had gone up the Sofenweg where one could enjoy a beautiful view of the city and the Rhine Valley. She had climbed 342 meters of the Heiligenberg and had continued to the summit to admire the ruins of the Basilica of Saint Michael at an altitude of 445 meters.

"You have a good memory," Jean observed. "You cited names and numbers that I would have forgotten a long time ago."

"When I travel, I try to visit places that are worth seeing and I take notes," answered Hilda. Sometimes, in the evenings, I read the notes I've taken which helps me remember; the ruins, castles, mountains, and valleys reappear in my mind and it's as if I take the trip a second time."

"Have you travelled much?" Jean asked.

"It seems to me I've already told you that I haven't; I have never left German territory. If I had a map in front of me of our homeland and I could trace with a pencil the furthest points I've gone in my life, I assure you they would not be very numerous. I would start with Berlin, which I have only visited once; from there I would trace down to Bamberg; next, my pencil would trace to the west to Wurzbourg and Frankfort, up to Rhyn. I would follow the Rhine up to Cologne and I would go back down to Karlsruhe. I would return towards the east towards Stuttgart and Augsbourg to Munich, and I would return to Nuremberg passing through Passau, Regensburg, and Bayreuth. There you are, all the practical knowledge I possess of our country's and the world's geography."

"So, it's the first time you're leaving Germany and you're making the trip all by yourself!"

"Yes," Hilda answered, "but don't forget that my brother is waiting for me at the other end of my voyage."

The train continued its course towards the west. Hilda became quiet, absorbed by her thoughts. Jean watched her in silence for a few minutes and found her even more beautiful. Suddenly, an unpleasant thought crossed his mind: would she have accepted the next day's rendezvous to be polite for fear of offending him? He proposed the encounter on the Hindenburg Bridge without knowing if he would even make it there. In fact, the evening he would spend in Manheim could bring events that would keep him from ever seeing Hilda again. In that case, she would only feel contempt and indifference for him when she learned the whole story.

"Fräulein," he said trying to find the words to express his thoughts as clearly as possible. "Fräulein, I have definitely decided to leave Manheim tomorrow, so, we could continue this trip together and you wouldn't need to travel alone. Only I need to tell you … … that is … … if you would like … … in case you have no intention of … …."

"You may be direct with me," answered Hilda encouragingly.

"I don't know if I've assumed too much." He said.

"Assumed too much? What do you mean? Tell me," she said.

"If you prefer that I don't accompany you for the rest of the trip, I will respectfully honor your wish to continue alone," he said.

He spoke these words pleadingly, almost imploringly and clumsily, and he dropped his head to hide the emotion he was feeling.

"It's possible that I will never have the chance to see you again, that we will part company tonight." he added.

"And about our meeting on the Hindenburg Bridge tomorrow, at 9:00. What do you think?"

He believed he could hear a slight amount of regret in the voice of his companion and he was joyful.

"If circumstances beyond my control keep me from getting there, would you hate me?"

"Of course not," she answered. "But, can you think of an alternate place we could meet if you can't make it to the bridge?"

In a quick gesture, he took Hilda's small hand in his and squeezed it; she didn't pull back. Their eyes met and she found something so profoundly sad in Jean's eyes that she took pity on him.

"Listen to me, Hilda," he said with difficulty. "No matter what happens, please don't judge me too severely."

"What could possibly happen? If you were stopped, you being a soldier, but dressed in civilian clothes, do you think I would judge you? No, of course not. You aren't a criminal or a thief."

He was struck by the young girl's last words and he could no longer look her in the eye.

"Although, I feel there must be something else," she pursued and asked, "Do you trust me?"

"Yes, I have total trust in you."

"So, tell me what is worrying you, Heinrich. Maybe I can help you somehow."

Her female curiosity was awakened. The fugitive had such a great desire to reveal his identity, but the idea that she would see him as a thief and despise him, stopped him from confiding in her.

"Not right now and please don't ask me anything else," he said pleading.

She lowered her eyes and looked like she was reflecting on the situation. He contemplated, admiring her figure, her lips; and when she raised her head, he blushed like a young boy who had just committed a misdeed.

"Do you know what I think?" She said absentmindedly.

"Oh, very clever, who knows what young women think?" he answered jokingly.

"In a couple of days, we will say goodbye, and we will never see each other again," she declared.

"Why?" He questioned.

"You will rejoin your regiment; I will meet up with my brother and I will return to Nuremberg. The war will continue and that will be it, we will never meet again."

"We can see each other again after the war."

"After the war!" she cried. "I am certain that you don't believe your own words. It's possible that you think that, at this moment, but in a couple of weeks, you won't even think about me again."

He looked her in the eye and answered with reserve: "If I'm still alive when the war ends, and you will permit me, I swear I will come and see you."

She was silent, and he understood that he hadn't succeeded in convincing her.

"Listen to me, Hilda," he went on, "You don't understand. You cannot possibly comprehend the difficult situation I find myself in right now. Naturally, it is because of the war that I am in this particular situation."

His desire to convince her was so strong, he couldn't find the right words and he was afraid he might confuse her even more. He was conscious of the fact that he was repeating a lot of the same things twice and desperately continued:

"I really can't explain, but maybe later you'll understand. If I try to explain now, you will probably not understand, but after the war you'll know that I'm being truthful."

"But you haven't told me anything, although you keep saying that you're telling me the truth and it's quite probable that you are," she said dryly. Considering all the lies he had told her, she was still so trusting, and he became so guilt-ridden.

She shrugged her shoulders and continued: "Besides, why are we talking about all this and why do you think it matters to me whether we see each other or not after the war?"

He wondered what the reason could be for the sudden change in attitude. He didn't recall having said anything that may have upset her.

She couldn't possibly know that he had lied about his identity, but now he was becoming sorry.

He finally fell silent… … his inner voice was telling him to be ashamed of having put himself in this situation that forced him to lie. He regretted very much not having told her the truth from the beginning. She seemed like such a kind young woman, and she was so amiable.

At the same time, he had feelings of joy in his heart. If Hilda was talking this way, it was almost certain to him that she had some affection towards him, maybe more than a little affection. But it was too soon for him to draw any conclusions. After all, he had only known the young German woman for a few hours.

The train would arrive momentarily at Mannheim and before he left his companion, he wanted to see the smile reappear on her face.

With a soft voice he said, "It might seem improbable that I would talk about seeing you again after the war, but that really is my intention. It's the least I can do after you have given me food when I was dying of hunger, and I always repay my debts."

He noticed that her face took on a bitter look.

"You were hungry and you're hungry now. Even though you've eaten only a small sandwich. I regret that you didn't eat more. Since it's this piece of bread that you owe me, you don't have a very large debt."

During the darkest hours of his captivity, Jean thought that his greatest concern in the future would be to have food to satisfy his hunger. He was astonished to realize that, a few hours after his escape, other problems would surface other than the need for nourishment.

"Oh! I owe you a lot," he said evasively. "When I get back home… … that is… … when I rejoin my regiment, I would like to write to you. Would you mind giving me your address?" She took a business card out of her bag and gave it to him.

"I don't have a business card in my wallet," he said hesitantly, "but if you have a piece of paper and a pencil, I will write it down for you." She handed him an address book and a pencil, and he wrote down his address on a blank page. She read it and looked at him questioningly.

"Jean Stassart! What are you saying? What a strange name."

"This is the address of the people in Belgium where I will be staying. My parents send their letters to this address because this way I get their replies much faster."

"What if you change quarters?" she asked.

"I will continue to keep in touch with these people and I will visit during my vacation."

CHAPTER EIGHT

Manheim! The train entered this large station as the other passengers walked toward the doors to exit the train. As it arrived, he had an uneasy feeling; Jean rose slowly from his seat. He seized the young girl's largest suitcase in his left hand. He looked at her helplessly; the atmosphere had suddenly filled with a feeling of supreme unknown imminent danger. She didn't notice the look of panic in his eyes and he took the other bag. In an instinctive movement, as if his rescue depended on it, he firmly took her right arm. She smiled at him and they walked toward the exit. They were the last people to leave the car.

They arrived before the door; The platform was quiet. As in the other stations, one could not distinguish what was going on other than what was happening beneath the lights. The rest of the platform was completely obscure. People would appear beneath the lights then disappear into the shadows.

Jean quickly took in everything visible in the station. At the exit, the light was a little brighter and what he saw there shocked him so much, he came to a complete stand still. Men in uniform were guarding the exit of the building, asking each person for their identity papers. Hilda was surprised that her travelling companion was not moving forward and she followed the young man's gaze. She saw what was going on and slowly nudged him forward.

"Come on, keep going," she said. "It's more than likely that they are still searching for the prisoner of war from Nuremberg."

"No doubt," he said.

But he didn't move.

His fate could play out in the next few moments and he didn't know how to address this threat. Instead of moving forward, he had unintentionally taken a step back. The lamp illuminated his face, revealing the anguish and distress he was feeling, and the young woman noticed the terror in his eyes and the beads of sweat on his forehead. As if frozen, he remained immobile, his eyes fixed on the exit and resistant to Hilda's gentle nudging as she insisted on urging him forward.

All at once, she understood. In an instant she remembered his misspoken words, the odd French word he had uttered, the description of the escaped POW that came close to matching his, and the possibility that he might not make their rendezvous on the Hindenburg Bridge. His eyes were fixed on those of the girl and what he read in them alarmed him. He realized that his identity was no longer a secret to her. There was no need for words; everything he needed to say, he could read by the shock in her eyes.

"So, it's you, the escaped prisoner of war, thief of all that money!"

She read the confirmation of her thoughts in the sad eyes of her companion. "Yes, it's me. We have become such good friends throughout this trip; in honor of our friendship, I beg you, please don't betray me."

Her expression changed. The look on her face was reassuring and somehow as tender as a caress. She touched his arm and simply said:

"Follow me."

He followed her, full of confidence; together they descended on to the platform. With a light step, as if they were taking a walk, she steered him along the railway cars in a direction opposite from the exit, and soon they were enclosed in darkness. He allowed her to guide him without a word, trusting her implicitly. She advanced sure footedly over the tracks, following the platform, winding around and between the cars. She seemed to know this part of the station very well.

At one instance, they heard steps but saw no one. Hilda and Jean were amongst the rails. She crouched, pulling down the fugitive's arm and he followed her example. His ear was close to her mouth and he heard her even breathing; she didn't show any sign of trouble or fear and he admired her coolness. They moved forward quickly and quietly as they renewed their course.

They finally reached a grove of trees; a light snowfall covered the ground. This place must not have been frequented much because there were no footprints. Hilda stopped.

"On the other side of this fence there is a street," she said. You jump over the fence and I will catch up with you in a few minutes, but before you jump, look around and make sure there is nobody in the area."

"Hilda," he said, his voice full of emotion.

"I don't know how to show you my gratitude … … …."

"Let's not waste any time," she said.

He made his way over the fence and when he jumped down the other side, she passed him the suitcase he had been carrying. The street was dark and silent; nothing revealed a human presence in the surroundings, he listened to the steps of the young woman, moving away quickly. His guardian angel was leaving him.

He walked across the street and waited for the return of his faithful companion. For the first time, he realized how truly cold it was and he began to shiver. The hunger which he had forgotten for the moment due to the circumstance was beginning to evoke images of abundant and succulent dinner menus.

He felt very alone… … terribly alone, tracked like a wild animal, and as miserable as a lost dog. He felt as though the millions of inhabitants of this detested land beneath his feet fought against him. They were his enemies and constituted threat and danger. Among all these millions, there was only one single person, a young woman, who extended him the hand of friendship and offered him her support in his misery.

An immense feeling of gratitude for her filled his heart and he decided, if he came through this ordeal safely, he would be devoted to her for the rest of his life. He would never be able to repay the debt he owed her. His misery was so immense, that he envisioned her as a princess or a queen who had placed her hand on the head of a beggar.

A few steps from him, the brightness from a streetlight shone on the pavement which still had a few traces of snow. Passersby were rare, but every time someone came into his circle of vision, he scrutinized them from under his hat. If per chance he were to be accosted by a policeman, he would try to use all his remaining strength to knock him down and then he would take flight.

He had lost all sense of time. It felt like such an eternity since he had left Hilda and it seemed that she had had so much time to return. Maybe she wouldn't come back; not that he could blame her; she had helped to get him out of a terrible situation, and he couldn't really ask for more. She had done an honorable thing for him and she had his total gratitude, even if she had decided to abandon him now.

The cold brought him back to a warm, safe place beside his parent's fireplace. This vision came to him many times as he sat in the barracks of the prisoner of war camp at Nuremberg. He had spent many hours dreaming of warming himself and having something to eat. Warmth and nourishment, the two most predominant struggles that life was handing him; he wasn't aware of any other desires.

A hesitant figure emerged from the veil of darkness and appeared under the light. Hilda! In a few long strides he found himself beside her.

"Come on over into the shadows," she said. She set the suitcase down against a wall and let out a big sigh: "we won't be noticed, and we can plan our next move."

"Hilda," he said, "I don't want you to get in any trouble on my account. I'll be grateful to you for the rest of my life for everything you've done for me, but at this point, we need to part. It's much too dangerous for you. From now on it's necessary for me to manage on my own. I will carry your suitcase up to your sister-in-law's house; it's the least I can do for you after all you have risked for me, but at this time, it's the only thing I'm capable of doing for you. After that, I'll leave you and I will continue my trip without you. For months now, I've had only myself to rely on all the time. I just hope I can survive, despite everything."

"But what will you do tonight? Under these conditions, you can't even go to a hotel. So, do you plan to spend the night under the stars in this frigid cold?"

He detected a touch of terror and pity in the voice of the young German and he was moved. They were so close to each other that Hilda's chest brushed against him and he felt a warm thrill in his heart, although the present situation was terrifying, he had tasted a few seconds of joy, unknown to him until now, elated that this young woman had such feelings for him.

She raised her eyes to him, and he detected a glow through the murkiness of the surroundings.

"Do you really think I could sleep, knowing that you were outside in this icy night? Oh, Heinrich!"

This cry from the young woman's heart touched the prisoner right down to his soul. In a low, bitter, sarcastic tone, he answered.

"My name is Jean Stassart, escaped prisoner of war and thief."

"You must have suffered terribly," she said with a sigh and tears in her eyes.

"I regret nothing," he said. "If I hadn't lived these long months in the prisoner of war camp, I would never have had the joy of knowing you. Now, pardon me for what I am about to tell you, and if I offend you, it certainly isn't my intention.

"It's possible that I will soon be apprehended, and I may never see you again… … and I want to promise you something."

He was silent for a moment, took her hands in his and continued.

"The hours I have spent with you on the train are among the happiest hours I have ever spent in my entire life. The weeks and months I'm facing could be most terrible for me, but I will always carry in my heart the image of the kindest, most gentle girl I have ever met… … although I don't understand why you would have any interest in my fate. I will think of you as a blessed angel until I draw my last breath."

He brought her hands to his lips and kissed them. Then he added, "I love you with all my heart, Hilda." She moved closer to him and he heard his name from a voice strangled by emotion.

"Jean!"

He took her gently into his arms and kissed her.

"I am so happy that you love me," she said. "I love you too."

He remained silent for a few minutes, drinking in the joy of holding her against him. "So," he said, "Holding you in my arms makes me very happy and almost makes my heart ache. I believe everything that I have endured as a prisoner of war has been compensated by the joy I feel right now. If I go back to hell tomorrow or later, I will know that I have been in heaven tonight."

"Would you do me a big favor?" she asked.

"You may ask me anything. I won't refuse you anything that's in my power to give you."

"I want you to accompany me to my sister-in-law's house and spend the night in a warm bed. I'm sure it's been a long time since you've slept on a soft mattress, between clean white sheets."

"I had long given up wishing for things that people take for granted, but I'm not sure I should accept. What will your sister-in-law say if you walk in with a total stranger? Worst case is that you are both exposed to great danger by giving asylum to a prisoner of war, thief, and fugitive."

"You are not a thief and we don't need to tell her anything. How would I know that you are a fugitive from a stalag? You speak our language very fluently; people could easily mistake you for a German. Don't worry about my sister-in-law, she won't suspect anything and she's a very charming hostess."

She left the comfort of her friend's arms.

"Now, we must leave quickly. My sister-in-law is expecting me, and she will worry if I arrive too late."

He retrieved her suitcase again but just when they were about to leave, she grabbed his arm.

"There are a lot of policemen around the train station," she said. "I don't understand why there are so many, and I don't believe that they have mobilized that many men just to find a POW, so there must be something else going on. In any case, we will take a small detour by the Schwetzingerstrasse and we will cut through the center of the city. I also think it would be most prudent to walk rather than take the tram, where there are a lot of policemen and members of the Gestapo who have your description by now." He took her by the arm, and they proceeded at a brisk pace. He felt very happy, as if he was a free man and he heard a constant murmur in his ears. She loves me. She loves me. And for a while, he had forgotten about the cold and his hunger pangs.

They soon reached the labyrinth of the center of the city, which is a grid plan formed by 136 rectangles, designated by letters and numbers. Hilda seemed to know this part of Mannheim very well; she advanced without pausing, crossing one street after the other, without hesitating. Finally, they arrived at the Parade-Plats. They turned left and followed this street for several minutes.

Along the way, Jean told the young woman how he had escaped and how he had accidentally gained possession of the money. He told her all this in a simple manner without hiding or omitting even the smallest detail. He even admitted that at some point he had thought of using her to succeed in his escape.

"I know you aren't a thief," she said simply.

At the corner of one street, she stopped.

"Here we'll take the street to the right; it's the Luisen-Ring. We will soon arrive at our destination."

A light at the corner of the street they had just left illuminated the name of the street.

The Rheinstrasse; it surprised him, *after all,* he thought, *we are in Ludwigshafen.*

"We are in Mannheim," said the young woman. "I have passed through here before, but I've never paid attention to the street names. Here we are fixed on this point: there is one Rheinstrasse in the two cities."

"Your sister-in-law will probably not be very happy. I've told you a lot of lies, but these circumstances have made me strong," he said sadly.

"Naturally, you wouldn't disclose your situation to just anyone you meet," she said. "It will be very comforting to arrive at my sister-in-law's place and sit by a warm fire."

"I suppose she'll be very surprised to see you accompanied by a stranger."

"She'll thank you for having taken care of me."

"Me, take care of you?"

"You'll see," she said with a giggle.

They walked warily. Passersby were very rare on the Luisen-Ring, partly because of the freezing temperature and because it was getting so late as well. After a few minutes, Hilda stopped and studied the surroundings.

"I think we need to go this way," she said, indicating a dark, gloomy street. They took this street and crossed a railroad track; and a little further down, they found themselves on the bank of a large river.

"The Neckar," said the young woman. "We are about five minutes from my sister-in-law's. We'll turn right, and we'll by-pass the river by taking the Friedrichs-Brucke."

The banks of the Neckar were deserted, and they reached Friedrichs-Brucke…
… they didn't encounter a single person. In the proximity of the bridge, they both came to a halt at the same time. The bridge was guarded by several men and under a streetlight stood an automobile whose occupants were controlling the area. This was a spectacle which Jean had witnessed many times during his journey and each time it was the subject of alarm and anxiety for him.

Hilda steered her companion to a dark area from where they could watch the men on the bridge. The engine of the control automobile started up and left and the sentinels on the bridge began to stamp their feet to keep warm.

"I think you were correct when you said that the police weren't mobilized just to find me," Jean said. "It's possible they're looking for me as far as Manheim, but there most certainly is something else going on that we aren't aware of."

He was quiet when he heard footsteps approaching. They noticed the silhouette of a man walking a few feet ahead of them, but Jean and his friend were well hidden in the shadows and remained unobserved. When the man disappeared, the fugitive again proceeded to talk.

"Again, my advice, and our only choice, is for you to go on to your sister-in-law's house as planned, and I will wander around these streets and blend in as best I can, until tomorrow morning. I'll see you tomorrow at 9:00 A.M. at the Hindenburg Bridge. If I'm not there by 9:15, you must assume that I've been captured, and you must leave without me."

"That is not an option! I implore you, it's useless to discuss. Not only that, I won't leave you behind. I don't want to suffer the anguish that I'll feel knowing that you're out here in the danger and the cold and that I may never see you again."

He knew from the sound of her voice that she was unyielding and would not leave him under any circumstance. He felt an odd sense of joy and anxiety at the same time. She must certainly love him, but what would they do now?

"If we follow the river down to the next bridge, chances are there wouldn't be any guards on it," he said.

"Don't fool yourself," answered Hilda with bitterness. "You can bet your life that the other bridges will be guarded as well."

What she said was logical. He could not cross the Neckar, but the thought of his companion spending the night outside in this weather with him was not a choice. He was used to misery and survival, but she was a young woman who had never been placed in such a trial of strength. He needed to make one final attempt to convince her.

"Listen to me," he continued unmoved, "you will go to your sister-in-law's house because she is expecting you and is probably worried by now and you cannot continue to expose yourself to this frigid weather and extreme danger if you're caught with me. I'm sure I can find a quiet area where I can spend the night, either by the rail road track we passed a few moments ago, or some dark alley with both entry and exit, in case I am found and I have to run."

"I will not abandon you!" she responded fiercely.

"You are the most self-sacrificing person I have ever known," he said, "but you have got to be reasonable. It would be of no benefit to either of us if you spent the night outside and something should happen to you or you got sick or God forbid, captured, and accused of being a traitor. I would never forgive myself."

"I have an idea!" interrupted Hilda, almost jubilantly. "There are barges on the Neckar and behind each barge there is a small boat. Don't you think we could cross the river on one of the boats? The helmsmen are probably asleep at this hour and from the bridge, nothing will look out of the ordinary because it's too dark on the water and we would be invisible."

She placed her hands on the shoulders of the fugitive, moved her face close to his and added a little hesitantly:

"Maybe it would be too demanding for you; you must be exhausted."

"That's worth trying," he said, "I'll take your suggestion, but I will go alone. I'll make it, I'm sure of it. When I feel weak, I'll think of you and it will give me strength. A man can endure much more than he thinks when that adrenalin kicks in: I've had that experience. I'm only upset because I'm causing you so many difficulties."

"Yes, you're causing me some anxiety, but if you get arrested, you'll cause me a lot of sorrow. Okay, I won't go with you across the river, but I will meet you on the other side. Now, let's not waste any more time talking. I will cross the bridge and you'll join me on the other side of the Neckar. We will count the steps from here to the bridge and you will come back to this spot to cross the river and I will count as many steps along the other side and find the approximate place we'll meet."

They embraced.

"Hilda, I love you. Let's go, but if I'm taken, promise me you will not recognize me and keep walking away from me." She reluctantly nodded her agreement.

After they walked to the Friedrichs-Brucke while counting their steps, he cautiously walked back to the spot they had selected and proceeded down towards the edge of the river.

CHAPTER NINE

White misty plumes of fog floated up from the water and a light, icy breeze chased them in the direction of the bridge. The river sank into deep darkness; a very uncertain and menacing situation for Jean. Sometimes the unknown is more frightening than reality.

The fugitive advanced to the left where the dark mass of a barge drew an unclear shape in the fog. The barge was very close to the dock, and Jean presumed the helmsman's cabin was there, but invisible behind the layer of fog. He could see another dark shape on the water which he took to be the smaller boat beside it. To verify, he felt around for a stone and dropped it on this spot. He heard a hollow sound – the stone had not fallen into the water indicating that the stone had hit the bottom of the boat – easing his tension; hopefully, the helmsman would not come to investigate the noise.

The difference between the upper level of the barge and the dock was more than a meter: the boat was lower. From the opposite side of the river, there was a brilliant light, which illuminated the surroundings and provided a guiding beacon to assist his crossing, however, it was impossible for the fugitive to estimate the width of the Neckar; was it 100 or 200 meters? He took one last furtive look around, but other than the silhouettes of the guards on the bridge, he could not distinguish any other human presence.

He knew it would take courage to achieve this crossing - a crossing presenting unexpected difficulties and dangers. But on the opposite bank the young woman he loved was waiting for him, a young German woman risking her life to save his.

He stretched out on the ground and slid down the side of the dock until his feet met some resistance… he was on the barge. He pressed against the wall listening carefully, his eyes trying to penetrate the night. All remained quiet. As stealthily as a wolf, he reached the back of the barge. He could just barely make out the boat and soon found the mooring chain; there wasn't much distance between the two. He descended alongside the barge and wrapped his legs and his hands around the chain which was covered by a thick layer of frost while watching to make sure he wasn't discovered. His fingers stiffened, but with all the strength he could muster from his weakened and exhausted body, he guided the small boat towards him with his feet. The effort produced a creaking noise and the craft swung dangerously from side to side. He ceased moving immediately, watching to make sure he wasn't spotted. He waited 10 minutes and proceeded.

In an instant, the fugitive was balancing over nothingness. He dropped to the boat below with a thud. It swayed twice and banged into the barge. Although the commotion was confined to a short distance, the strained nerves of the young man thought it sounded much louder than it really did. The helmsman must either be a very sound sleeper or drunk to not be disturbed by the noise.

His feet landed in the frigid water at the bottom of the boat and he pulled them out quickly. At the same time his head felt unusually cold and he realized he had lost his hat. He was shivering and his teeth chattered.

He began immediately to look for his headgear, fearing that if it was found, it might establish his presence in the area.

Two or three times, his hands went in the water and he soon abandoned the search. His fingers felt like ice and he was afraid he would not have any use of them or be too weak to accomplish the crossing. He grabbed the mooring rope that tied the barge and boat together and slid his hands down until he found the knot. In vain, he tried to undo the knot, the frost had intensified, and his fingers were so stiff from the cold that they refused to cooperate. His whole body was quivering. The tension which had seized him licked his forehead with large drops of sweat and his breath left his mouth with great whistling noises.

After a few attempts without any results, the idea came to him to rub the rope to remove the frost and make it a little less frosty and slippery. The white matter soon melted, but the water that it produced stiffened his fingers so much that the fugitive was forced to stop.

He dried his hands by rubbing them on his clothes, and then instinctively, he put the tips of his fingers in his mouth to warm them. The abrupt change between the intense cold and the warmth was so painful that despite all his impatience, he was obliged to wait until his fingers returned to normal.

As he waited, his hands in the sleeves of his coat, he detected the sound of footsteps on the barge. He crouched down in the rowboat, looking towards the sky. The sound of the steps came closer and he could see the silhouette of a man standing near the helmsman's cabin. Jean's heart was beating so rapidly you would think the man could hear it. The man looked over the side of the barge, tossed his cigarette, spat into the water, then turned, coughed, and walked away.

The fugitive waited a few minutes until he felt it was safe to move, then, clenching his teeth, and mustering all his strength, he again tried to untie the knot. He finally succeeded after several attempts, despite his aching fingers. He again plunged his feet into the frigid water of the boat. He seized the oar while putting all his weight against the wall of the dock. The rowboat slid silently into the river. The oar was very heavy, and it was extremely hard for him to row, exacerbated by hunger and fatigue. Soon, he was sweating and breathing heavily as a horse running a series of laps around a racetrack.

The Neckar was wide in this area and except for the lights from the bridge; he couldn't see anything around him, but the lights did help him get oriented. He advanced cautiously for fear of propelling the boat against a barge or in case a helmsman might notice its presence on the river. First, he was surprised by the size of the Neckar, then he concluded that the slow speed with which he had rowed, and the river current might be the cause of the length of the crossing seeming to take so much time.

Finally, a large object loomed before him in the darkness; it was another barge. The young man believed he was finally on the other side of the river. He reduced the speed of the boat and slid between two other rowboats. After listening attentively for any telltale sounds, he rose to his full height, and extending his hands above his head, he found he could reach the rail around the barge and hoist himself up. When his feet were firmly on the deck, he felt like he had exhausted what remained of his strength and he sat on a bench and remained seated for a moment to catch his breath. Weakness kept him there, increasing the danger of being detected. His despair was so great that he felt apathetic to anything that could still happen to him, unable to make a move. All the joints in his body ached and his fingertips were bleeding. Yet, in his mind, an image appeared of this young German girl whom he loved and who was waiting for him on the other side of the river and he became re-energized. He got up and walked to the wall of the dock on the other side of the barge. The ground's level was approximately at the height of the top of his head. He began to climb, but the freezing water on the wall was making it very slippery; he had nothing to hang on to. His feet found no support and he relied on the strength of his arms to raise his body up to the dock. Falling now, could result in serious injury.

After many excruciating efforts and a frantic will sustaining him, he finally reached the top of the wall. He painfully raised himself, injured knees and elbows, and walked unsteadily to the river's bank knowing that he had to leave this area immediately, not even rationalizing how he would accomplish it.

He let out a small yell when he felt someone taking his arm; he turned and saw Hilda.

"You startled me," he said breathlessly. "My nerves, you understand."

"I was worried," she said with compassion. "It took far too long for you to cross the river. Was it difficult? You're all wet, where's your hat? What happened?"

"Yes, it was very difficult," he said, breathing heavily and ignoring her other comments. "There is one point where I thought I wouldn't make it." He shivered and did up his coat.

"But you see, I have succeeded anyway," he said wearily.

They walked slowly, she took his arm and unconsciously, he leaned on her heavily. The need to rest governed his mental state and without the presence and support of his companion, he would have dropped to the ground and fallen asleep from exhaustion.

She felt his weight as he leaned against her and she understood that he was in a weakened condition.

"You must be terribly hungry," she said. "Tell me what you've eaten today."

"Just a crust of bread this morning in the barracks of the stalag and then you gave me a sandwich on the train. If you could get me something to eat, I'll pay you." A sudden thought crossed his mind.

"I would pay you with my money, not with the money I stole inadvertently."

"In a few moments we will arrive at my sister-in-law's and you will be able to eat. Don't concern yourself with anything else, or I will lose my sense of humor." The young woman's kindness touched him deeply.

"Hilda," he said, his voice trembling with emotion. "Hilda, I will be grateful to you until my dying day for everything you've done for me. I cannot express the gratitude I feel in my heart; I love you and will love you forever. If it's in the stars that our destinies must join, I will spend the rest of my days making you as happy as I can."

"There is nothing in the world that will make me happier than your love," she answered. "However, don't talk so much about your gratitude, and stop thanking me." We have more pressing things to think about.

In a moment, she stopped in front of the door of a house and rang the doorbell. Almost as soon as she stepped back, the door opened, and a woman appeared.

"Well, here you are, finally!" a joyous voice cried out. "I've been wondering what had happened to you … … but, you're not alone."

Hilda hugged the woman.

"I'll explain all that later. Let's go in first and get warm; it's colder than the devil out here and I'm starved. I hope you don't mind me bringing along a guest."

They followed the woman into a small, clean, warm kitchen.

"You must both be frozen; go and sit by the fire," said Hilda's sister-in-law cordially.

"My friend, Heinrich Lutz," The young German woman introduced Jean. "I had lost my bag with all my money in it; Heinrich found it and returned it to me."

Then, addressing Jean, who was stupefied at the ease with which she had spoken these lies, she continued.

"Martha Korber, my brother's wife."

Jean shook the hand which Martha Korber extended. He guessed that she was around 25 years of age, quite plain, an immediate pleasant expression, with an accommodating cordiality. She stared at the young man in wonder and Jean understood why.

"I'm pleased to make your acquaintance," he said with a pale smile and tired features. "I've entered your home in a rather rude and disrespectful manner. I must therefore apologize for my appearance and I fear that I'm making a mess of your tidy kitchen."

He looked down at his soaked shoes and continued:

"I walked out on some ice which wasn't solid enough to support my weight; and I got my feet all wet and fell; maybe it taught me a lesson." Trying to keep the conversation light, he said, "When I was a child, I was always testing the ice to see if it was solid and I'm afraid the habit has stuck with me."

"Remove your shoes, sir, I'll let you wear my husband's slippers," said Martha.

She passed them to him, and Hilda took the overcoat off her friend's shoulders. He seated himself near the fire while Martha took her sister-in-law's bags, then the two women disappeared into the next room and the fugitive heard Martha whisper:

"He looks so exhausted; it shows on his face. He looks like he hasn't slept in several nights. I wonder where he comes from."

"He seems very honest, after all, he didn't steal the money in my pocketbook, he could easily have gone on his way and kept it." answered Hilda.

They returned from the kitchen and Martha began to slice some bread. She put two bottles of beer and a plate of sausages on the table and politely invited Hilda and her companion to have some food.

The young woman chewed slowly, staring intently at the prisoner of war. She noticed that he was devouring the bread and the meat with the appetite of a voracious beast. He never once raised his eyes. Hilda remembered hearing that the prisoners of the stalag suffered greatly from hunger, but she had never paid any attention because she wasn't really interested; not only that, she had never believed these stories. Now she began to understand that these rumors had some truth to them. That's why the prisoners of war begged for bread from the people they worked with, and why they exchanged some of their non-essential clothing for a bit of nourishment.

Tears welled up in her eyes as she began to understand how her companion must have suffered over the last few months, but he was too preoccupied with his food to notice. However, Martha noted the sadness in Hilda's face, and she sensed that her sister-in-law had a great deal of affection for the young man.

He finished his meal, perspiring and a bit embarrassed.

"Please excuse me," he said, "I was terribly hungry, and I believe I have eaten more than is polite, but I will pay you for the food."

"Of course not, there's no question," answered Martha. Then, addressing her sister-in-law, she said:

"So, thanks to this gentleman, you got your bag and your money returned to you? Tell me about it."

"Yes," said the young woman. "As I began to exit the train station, there was a lot of activity from the policemen asking for ID and when I reached for my bag to get it, I realized that I must have left my pocket book inside the compartment of the train. I returned and boarded the train and I checked the car I had occupied and found nothing. I questioned the employees one after the other to see if they had found it, when suddenly I came face to face with Heinrich. I recognized him as the gentleman who had occupied the same compartment as I had. I've been looking for you for about fifteen minutes," he said. "Here is your bag. You left it on the train."

"Lucky for you," observed Martha, "your trip to Belgium would have been impossible if you hadn't found it. Suppose someone else had found your papers."

"As a matter of fact, Heinrich is on his way to Aix-la-Chapelle and he missed his train while trying to find me, so, I invited him to spend the night here; I hope that's not a problem."

"Certainly," confirmed Martha, noting that Hilda was calling him by his first name. "If you hadn't, I certainly would have scolded you, my dear."

"But what is happening here, in Manheim?" the young woman asked, changing the subject. "The train station is teeming with policemen and they are strictly monitoring the passengers and the pedestrians on the streets are also being asked for I.D. There are even patrols on the Neckar Bridge."

"Last night, an English plane crash landed in a field somewhere in the vicinity. Two or three of the occupants jumped out by parachute and they're searching for them all over the region." Martha said excitedly.

"Oh! That's all?"

Martha Korber glanced surprisingly in the direction of her sister-in-law.

"You thought it might be worse?" she said surprised.

"No, but I saw George Krahl at Heilbronn where authorities were searching for a prisoner of war who escaped from the stalag at Nuremberg. I thought that's what was going on here. By the way, George said he will arrive in Mannheim before noon tomorrow."

"So, we can expect him to visit, since you're here," said Martha, laughing.

"He is annoying," said Hilda shrugging her shoulders. "As far as I'm concerned, he doesn't need to stop in here."

"The poor, young man! He loves you so," said Martha in a half mocking half serious tone.

The young woman looked at Jean, but he had his eyes fixed on the stove in front of him and he seemed not to be paying much attention to the conversation.

"He gets more unbearable by the minute," said Hilda. "But you haven't told me how my brother is."

"The last letter I received from Rudolf is dated about two weeks ago," she replied, with her voice losing its pleasure. "He hoped to come home on leave next month, to see little Elizabeth. It's been ten weeks now since he's been home."

"Come on! Let's be a little optimistic and have a little patience," said Hilda as she stood. "This war won't last forever; I'm sure it will be over by the end of the summer. You'll see, and you will be extremely proud of your soldier when he returns victorious. Not only that, but little Elizabeth will know her father is a hero."

Martha lowered her head.

"Oh! I wish so much that Rudolph was here, I miss him so much," she said. "I know that Germany will win this war, at any cost. Nevertheless, sometimes, I feel so sad because of my husband's absence."

Then, in a lower tone of voice and in a tone of hopelessness, she added: "You know, Hilda, I sometimes have moments of weakness and then I feel apathetic to whether we win the war or not. No matter what happens, I hope Rudolph returns safely and in good health. They can ask me to make any sacrifice for the good of Germany, but not the life of my husband."

"Don't think those dark thoughts," answered the young woman, "and please don't talk like that. You wait and see. Rudolf will come back; I've always convinced myself of that in my own mind. Besides, the Wehrmacht (Unified Armed forces of Nazi Germany) is not suffering any losses at this moment and England will soon be unable to sustain the terrible attacks that our Air Force is inflicting on them daily. The English will soon be brought to their knees and they will be begging for peace."

She gave Martha a few friendly taps on the shoulder and said in a tone of encouragement: "I will probably see my brother the day after tomorrow and I think I'll find that his thoughts are totally different from yours. We'll talk about you and Elizabeth and he will tell me that you need to have a little more patience and a little courage. Just look forward to seeing him if he gets his vacation in a few days and see if I return with him."

"He wrote me that he is staying with some nice people," said Martha as if talking to herself. "They say that Belgians are very good people, right?"

"They are also kind, pleasant people. I've been by the POW camp at Nuremberg last summer. At that time, they were still lodging the prisoners in tents. I took pity on them; they seemed so quiet and so resigned to their plight. It must be so hard to be a prisoner of war!"

She let out a heavy sigh.

"We should probably cease our conversation," said Martha. "You two must be very tired and our chatter is keeping you from getting some rest. Hilda, would you please show Heinrich to the first bedroom? I prepared the room for you, but you can sleep with me tonight."

"Yes, but first I would like to go in and see Elizabeth," said Hilda.

Jean said goodnight to his hostess and followed the young woman to the stairs. She pushed open a door, turned on the light, and steered the fugitive towards a crib. A baby was sleeping in it with closed fists. Hilda kissed one of the little hands and said smiling, "She is beautiful, isn't she?"

"Yes," said Jean thoughtfully. "A peaceful and very tranquil look on her little face." Then silently, he wondered what her fate will be. *Will she also know such troubled times as we are experiencing?*

"Every human being has his joys and sorrows, hopes and dreams. But it's not always the same with everyone. Some are more sensible than others. Even in the same circumstances, a particular effect or event has a different impact on one person than on the other."

She turned towards him and resumed: "I would like to know what happened to your hat; I asked you before, but you didn't give me an answer."

"It fell into the waters of the Neckar during the crossing, but that's not important."

"I hope not. Now, I'll show you to your room."

She turned out the light and closed the door to the sleeping child's room. She opened another door and turned on the light.

"Here you are," she said, with a smile. "Are you pleased with it?"

"It's a dream," he assured her, glancing at the small clean room and the bed. "I owe you so much, Hilda, and you probably don't have any idea of the impact of what you're doing. Do you realize that you're actually betraying your own country for me?"

"I'm not betraying my country, since you're not a danger to my homeland. It's only the police who can accuse me and then only until your innocence is established."

He took her hands in his.

"At first, I was so impatient to see my parents and my village again," he said seriously. "But now everything has changed. I would ignore everything for you, and I would prefer to stay in Germany with you, rather than return to Belgium without you."

"No," she answered in fear, "you have to return to see your parents. You can't stay here, you'll be captured and… …."

She stopped and turned her face toward the young man.

"I would not rest or have any peace if you were arrested; I know they would treat you very cruelly. I don't want anything to happen to you and I want to accompany you as far as the country of your birth. Please don't refuse me that."

"I wouldn't refuse you anything, but I would never forgive myself if something happened to you because of me," he said. "If we should manage to cross the border, I would introduce you to my parents and then… … …"

"Then?"

"Then, I would ask you again if you still loved me and I would ask you to be my wife. I don't need to get to know you any better; I already know what a good and kind person you are."

He took her in his arms and kissed her and they were locked in an intense embrace and they forgot everything but this moment. The world, in its misery, the dangers and menaces, all disappeared and only their love triumphed over everything.

"I didn't know that any human being could be so happy," sighed Jean.

"Everything is different now. There's only one thing that's important to me, and that is you," said Hilda.

A little later, as he closed the bedroom door, the fugitive listened to the sound of the young woman's retreating footsteps, thinking of nothing but the object of his love, and everything else was forgotten. He got into bed and fell asleep immediately, but he wasn't to have a very restful sleep; he was haunted by dreams and all through the night, he had nightmares of the grave danger he and his friend were in. He was dreaming of Hilda being surrounded by an angry crowd throwing stones and yelling insults and she was being chased from her home. When he reached her, her face was all bloodied and almost unrecognizable. She walked, with unseeing eyes staring straight ahead, and as he tried to protect her, he felt a sharp blow. He fell with a loud cry, like a bull that has been slaughtered. The cry woke him up; he struggled a moment to figure out where he was, and immediately went back to sleep.

Another vision haunted his sleep. He was in the barracks of the stalag, alone, stretched out on the cot. It was very dark, and he stared at the small window across the room. There were barbed wires, behind which he saw Hilda's bloodstained face. She was rubbing her face against the barbed wire and was calling in a plaintive voice, "Save me, save me, save me!"

Fear kept him glued to the straw; he was incapable of making a move, and always the plaintive voice kept repeating the same words: Save me! Save me!

He let out a cry of terror. "No!" The bloodstained face continued to rub against the barbs of the barbed wire and she continued her appeal. Then he saw the hands of the young woman which seemed to press against the window. He wanted to yell: Go away! But fear paralyzed his tongue as well as his body…. at this point, he awoke again, relieved that this was only a nightmare.

"I'm just not used to sleeping in such a comfortable bed," he said to himself.

He fell back into a restful sleep and his slumber was no longer troubled.

CHAPTER TEN

He woke up in the late morning. Thin rays of daylight streamed into the room through the blinds. Immediately, the smiling face of his young friend came to mind and he relived every instant he had spent in her company since his departure from Nuremberg, until their passionate embrace before he went to bed.

A new day was beginning, a day which presented serious events which would decide the success or the failure of his dangerous scheme.

He got out of bed and opened the blinds. It was snowing and there was a thick covering on the rooftops of the houses and on the road. His body shivered and he shrugged off a sense of foreboding and he forced himself to think about Hilda and soon the desire to see her eliminated all his troublesome thoughts.

He proceeded to the bathroom and when he looked in the mirror, he noted that he needed a shave; his beard was beginning to show, which might make him look suspect. He made a mental note to take advantage of the time he had left before leaving for the border to locate a barber.

He went down to the kitchen and found Hilda, Martha, and little Elizabeth in the deliciously warm kitchen. He greeted them and told his young friend of his wish to get a shave.

After breakfast, Jean and Hilda left together. The young girl pointed out a barber shop and the fugitive entered. There were no other clients and the barber immediately began to work. He was in his fifties and a talker, as are all the people in his line of work. He spoke about the hard times and the current events: the times were bad; the events were favorable to Germany, and without a doubt, the Reich would win the war. We would see the colonial empire of Germany revitalized in greater scope than she had ever been, even greater than the colonial British empire.

Jean responded as briefly as possible, although he hated to pretend to share the opinions of the barber. He felt that the less he said the less the barber would guess that he was a stranger to Mannheim. The barber also took the opportunity to tell the story of the British plane shot down near the city. He said he was sure the occupants would be arrested very quickly; just as surely as the water of the Rhine flowed into the sea.

He then told the story that the previous evening, he had the occasion to walk along the Neckar where he had gone to cut a client's hair that was very ill. As he passed by the river, he saw a crowd of people on the bank and he approached them to see what was going on. The police had fished a hat out of the river which had apparently belonged to a poor unfortunate wretch who had fallen into the river. It's dangerous to wander during the night; it's not like it was before the war, when the streets were well lit, and you could see almost as well at night as you could during the day. Now, since the war had started, the cities had to be kept dark at night and everyone was ordered to keep their blinds closed to prevent the threat of enemy planes flying overhead and making out cities below that they could bomb.

Jean didn't say a word while the barber talked about the hat, but in the meantime, he was happy that his shave was complete. As he exited the shop, he noticed it was still snowing. He directed his steps towards the house of Rudolf Hessling, when he saw Hilda cross the street waiting to join him.

"Surely you haven't been waiting for me in the cold." He asked.

"Yes, I have," she answered. "I don't want to lose sight of you as long as you are on my soil."

"You are my guardian angel."

He offered her his arm and she took it and they made their way slowly in the snow. The whiteness of the snow reflected favorably on Hilda's face, giving her a lovely glow.

"The barber told me that a hat had been retrieved from the waters of the Neckar. They think someone has accidentally fallen into the river. They are probably searching right now for a cadaver. So, we are good up to this point; my old hat will not give me away."

"I hope not," replied Hilda, and Jean was reminded that she had already talked about the same subject earlier.

"I don't think so?" he insisted.

"Listen to me, Jean," she said. "I know a man on the police force, George Krahl, who I have spoken to you about before. He has told me a few stories about some of the cases he and his colleagues have encountered; I want to tell you these people are very intelligent and persistent. They have a lot of experience and when they are on somebody's trail, it's rare that one escapes. I'm not trying to discourage you, far from it; I just want to remind you to be very careful. I will help you as much as I can and I pray for the success of your operation, but we must, I repeat, be very prudent."

"I planned this escape in a moment of nostalgia and despair," declared Jean. "I thought it through before I did it and I anticipated that there was a good chance I would succeed. But now I understand that without your help, I would already have been arrested."

"Do you still have that money? It's a bit careless to keep it in your pocket. If you were to be searched for one reason or another, they will know where it came from and it won't take long to discover your identity."

"In fact, you're right. I've already thought of that. I'm not really sure of the best way to get rid of that damned money."

"I have a proposition for you." She said.

"I'm listening! I've been very good at following your advice." He said.

"You can give me the money and I will make sure it gets to the rightful owner, without him knowing where it came from."

"How will you cross the border with this money?"

"I won't take it with me to Belgium. There is a small attic at my sister-in-law's where she stores all kinds of old items and she rarely goes up there. I'll hide it in the attic."

"You think of everything," said Jean, with an amusing smile. "If you were a thief sought by the police, you would have caused your friend George Krahl and his men a lot of problems. Open your bag and I'll slip this wallet in it."

"I have another point to draw your attention to," resumed Hilda. "When we get back to my sister-in-law's house, it's very likely that George Krahl will be there. Will you be able to keep your cool if he talks to you?"

"Of course, without a doubt."

"You know that policemen are very suspicious, and I know George. I'm sure he will ask you some questions."

"I hope he won't make me undergo an interrogation."

"I don't think he will, but I'm sure he will ask some questions during the conversation. Just be on your guard. He's extremely curious; he will without question want to know who is accompanying me and under what circumstances we have gotten to know each other. Remember what I told Martha about how we met. As for your identity, if he poses that question and asks you about your trip, tell him what you told me yesterday on the train, but try to stay away from any discussion about your military life. If I notice that you're getting uncomfortable, I will join in the conversation and try to change the subject."

When they returned to her brother's house, she rang the doorbell and Martha opened the door. She hugged Hilda and said laughing, "I told you he'd be here."

Jean, as well as Hilda, knew who she was referring to. Nevertheless, Hilda asked: "Who are you talking about?"

"Well, George Krahl, of course. When I told him you had gone for a walk with a friend, he asked me a ton of questions about your friend and he said that the weather wasn't really suitable for leisurely walks."

They entered and found themselves before a blond young man approximately Jean's age, a bit shorter, scrawnier, and due to his diet at the POW camp, a bit heavier than Jean. He had a naïve expression, but intelligent eyes. The fugitive had a good first impression of the policeman; he found him to be friendly and he regretted having to regard him as an enemy.

"So, did you have a good trip?" cried Hilda cheerfully as she shook his hand.

"If you had accompanied me, the voyage would have been much more enjoyable," replied George Krahl.

"For you maybe, but not for me. You would have bored me all the way with your many tales. I would like to introduce you to my friend, Heinrich Lutz. I suppose Martha has told you about him and you have probably wanted to know how I made his acquaintance."

She turned towards Jean and continued: "This is George Krahl, the most famous detective in the Reich." She said laughing.

The two men shook hands; the policeman looked the fugitive straight in the eye. Jean returned the look and he understood that the other perceived him as a possible rival as far as Hilda was concerned, but he seemed not to be aroused by any other suspicions.

"Friends of Hilda's are also friends of mine," said George.

"I'm honored to include you among my friends," Jean lied.

Hilda placed herself between the two men and turned to the policeman.

"Your escaped prisoner, have you arrested him?"

"Not yet, but we will."

"Also, the British airmen, are they still at large?"

"We have not found them yet, but I'm sure we will find them soon and they will be arrested. It's only a matter of time."

George Krahl spoke in a calm, positive voice with a tone of absolute confidence. The few words he had spoken, convinced the fugitive that George had an infinite confidence in the power of the organization to which he belonged. Jean was conscious of his self-assurance and he was beginning to feel a bit discouraged.

"Ah! But what are the police doing?" cried the young woman.

"They're doing everything possible," retorted George. "Sometimes it takes time to accomplish a mission they are entrusted with, but it always comes to a satisfactory end. Rest assured, we are doing our homework."

"So now your homework consists of stopping a poor prisoner of war whose nostalgia has made him run away from the cold barracks," remarked Hilda with some contempt.

"Our job consists of completing the orders we are given," answered the police-man, in the same calm tone, but rather coldly. "We are told to capture an escaped prisoner who is also a thief. We don't question his motives; there is another branch of our organization who deals with that. Our job is completed at the time of the in-dividual's arrest."

Obviously, George Krahl was very proud of the police force he was part of and despite the calm with which he spoke, he was visibly irritated at the slightest criticism of his duty.

"I detest your methods and I'm happy that my brother is not a policeman," de-clared the young woman.

"There you go," intervened Martha, "you've just barely seen each other, and the arguments begin. As for me, I like the stories you tell now and then, George. Tell me, is there anything new?"

"I'm allowed to reveal a few things, even though there is a critic of the police among us," he said with a mocking glance toward Hilda. I'm not in charge of the British pilot's case; it's the prisoner of war's case that I'm responsible for. I was warned at Heilbronn and I went to the train station to await the train's arrival from Nuremberg. We searched the train but there was no trace of the fugitive."

He raised his eyes to the ceiling thoughtfully and murmured, "Extremely strange."

"What's so strange about it?" inquired Martha.

"He was supposed to be on that train, but I'm sure we'll find an explanation to this setback. The case is nearing its end."

"What do you mean?" asked Hilda sharply.

"The fugitive is on the verge of being arrested."

The silence that followed his words was oppressing for Jean and his young friend. Martha looked at the officer with respect and seeing the effect produced by his state-ment on the others, George continued, plainly savoring his triumph.

"We are certain this individual is in Mannheim."

Hilda let out a small "Oh!" of surprise and perhaps terror also. The fugitive gave her a quick look and he noticed she had visibly paled in color. He himself found his throat to be very dry. George Krahl enjoying what he believed was amazement on the part of the girl, smiled and added: "What I have just told you is probably not en-tirely correct. However, I want to tell you, that the fugitive is either in Mannheim or in the vicinity. In any case, he was in the city last night."

Jean had the feeling that a slight air of relief had taken place in the oppressive at-mosphere of the kitchen and Hilda also felt a sense of relief.

"How do you know?" asked Martha, burning with impatience to find out more of the story.

"You know, for us, the smallest detail is often of paramount importance," said the officer a little boastfully. "There are certain things that, at first sight, may not have any importance, but sometimes these trivial things can be our biggest tip-offs and can generally put us on the right track.

"In the case before us, this small detail is in the form of a hat that was fished out of the waters of the Neckar. This hat is the one worn by the prisoner of war. It was stolen in the office of the stalag, in Nuremberg, at the same time as the overcoat and the wallet containing a great amount of money. We were almost certain that he had taken the train to Mannheim. He could have taken the one for Wurzbourg or went on foot, but we rejected the latter idea because it would not have been possible, unless it were summer. What we don't know, is if he stayed in Mannheim last night or if he continued on towards the Belgian border."

He uttered all these phrases like a professor who is teaching a class to his students. Jean found him to be a bit ridiculous at this moment, but he listened without raising his eyes, for fear that a look or a movement could raise the officer's suspicion, if it hadn't already.

"How do you know that it's the prisoner of war's hat?" inquired Hilda in such a tranquil voice that the fugitive couldn't help but admire the levelheadedness with which she spoke.

George Krahl, flattered by the interest the tale was creating, continued in the tone of someone who was reporting to his superiors on a mission which had ended in success.

"The initials of the owner of the hat, as well as the brand and address of the milliner, were inside the hatband. There is no doubt. However, there are several things in this whole business that are unclear to me right now, but that may be fairly simple to figure out."

"What don't you understand?" questioned Martha, who was listening with interest.

"First of all, the reason why the prisoner of the stalag interrupted his trip to come to Mannheim, when he could have continued his trip to Belgium, which should most certainly have been his goal, since he is a Belgian soldier.

"Instead of doing that, he ran the risk of leaving the Mannheim Handelshafen, which was well guarded by the police due to the ongoing investigation to find the British airmen. He must have had a good reason to do so and I am also sure that he couldn't have done it without help. Furthermore, considering all the security at the train station, how he would have left that location without being detected. It's almost impossible that he could have obtained false papers in the camp in Nuremberg because he had no means at his disposal. He did not use the papers that were in the wallet that he stole. The guards were warned that he might do this and if he had, he would have been arrested immediately. In any case, I think that this man is very clever; he must have created a very good escape plan."

He took out a package of cigarettes, offered one to Jean, who accepted it, and after lighting it he continued: "Since we don't understand what the prisoner was planning to do in Manheim, there are a few other things that we haven't been able to clear up.

I told you earlier that his goal to visit Mannheim escapes us, unless he knows someone here. Obviously, he didn't come here on a sightseeing trip. There are Belgian workers in various factories all over the city. He would likely know if a friend or a family member is in Mannheim and maybe he has come to seek some help from this person or persons. Could he have an accomplice?"

"There is no doubt," said Martha.

"I'm not as certain as you are," replied George Krahl with an indulgent smile. "This person may have received a visit from the fugitive without knowing what he is guilty of and even; perhaps, unaware that he is a prisoner of war. What we know beyond a doubt, is that he must know the city and has spent the night somewhere in the Neckarstadt. The hat which we found is convincing proof of that."

"Maybe he drowned," objected Martha.

"No, there is not a single man on the police force who would admit to this supposition and our fugitive did not throw his hat in the water on purpose to make us believe that he committed suicide. We also don't believe he fell in the water by accident.

"He is intelligent enough to know that this hat would create a clue for us. Besides, we have not found a body anywhere on the banks or in the water of the Neckar. He simply lost his hat as he was crossing the river and he has vanished into thin air. I believe he has accomplished this crossing in a launch belonging to a boatman because he has not crossed any of the bridges. They were all very well guarded and he would have been arrested."

"How do you know he crossed the river by rowboat?" Martha demanded again.

"A boatman's dinghy was found two kilometers from the barge to which it attaches and on the opposite bank."

George Krahl thoughtfully blew out a puff of smoke from his cigarette and added as if talking to himself: "The crossing of the Neckar must have been very hard for the man. I wonder how he managed to scale the walls along the riverbank, they were covered with a layer of ice, making it impossible to climb with his hands or his feet. I assure you, this was a skillful feat, a superhuman test of courage for a man in the weakened state he must have been in."

"This is an exciting story," said Hilda, mockingly, despite the discomfort she was feeling. "If ever you decide to write a crime novel, it would certainly be a best seller. Certainly, neither Arthur Conan Doyle nor Edgar Wallace would have done better, and the title would certainly attract fans of the genre, *Pursuit of a Man Across Germany.*"

"When are you leaving?" questioned George Krahl, changing the subject.

"This afternoon. I would like to arrive in Cologne to catch the night train to Brussels."

"Very well then, I would like to offer you a ride to the train station."

"You forget that I have a companion, my dear George!"

The policeman bit his lip and as he raised his eyes, they met those of Jean's. During a few brief moments, an idea crossed both men's minds. They seemed to wonder if instead of becoming friends, they would soon become rivals. Then the fugitive spoke: "I'm sorry if my presence prevents you the pleasure of accompanying your friend, in that case, you're more than welcome to take my place."

He pronounced the word "friend" with the intention of flattering the arrogance or self-esteem of George Krahl and at the same time let him think that the young woman had talked about George in favorable terms. Above all, he did not want the German policeman to become his enemy. Meanwhile, before George had a chance to respond, Hilda intervened with a charming smile addressing him: "I said all this to tease you, George, and I was about to ask you to accompany me, if you aren't on duty, of course."

The policeman chatted with the young woman until the clock chimed 12 noon. The conversation was kept light and cheerful thanks to Hilda and Jean, the latter being a little astonished at his young friend's self-control. A hint of jealousy entered his heart. The young German seemed to be oblivious to the presence of her travel companion. The words of a long forgotten French song came to mind:

"Quand tu viens me froler ta gaitee me fait mal et ta joie une souffrance." (When you come close to me the feeling of joy almost hurts and the joy makes me ache.)

George Krahl, to whom the girl had never shown such kindness, radiated this joy. When George left the house, Hilda remained silent for some time and Jean observed her thoughtful face with curiosity. She took advantage of her sister-in-law's absence to say to her companion: "I'm sure everything will work out well at the station this afternoon. Don't worry about it."

CHAPTER ELEVEN

When he saw the waters of the Neckar again, Jean was surprised to see that the river was so narrow. Crossing it the previous night, the tributary of the Rhine seemed much broader, at least several hundred meters wide, but that might have been because it was such a struggle to cross. He relived every phase of his adventure and knew that this was the hardest and most difficult risk he had ever undertaken.

Riding on the tram that led the fugitive, the young woman, and the policeman to the station at Ludwigshafen, Jean did not participate in the conversation. The other two chattered and laughed nonstop and Hilda seemed as carefree as a young girl with nothing on her mind leaving him a little envious.

Regardless of the Hilda's reassuring words earlier, Jean's mind was entirely preoccupied by the problems that could present themselves by this situation. Yet he was convinced that seeing Hilda focusing her attention on George might facilitate his venture.

They crossed the bridge over the Rhine, suspended high over the river they could see the waters carrying flows of ice in a northerly direction where the watery ribbon was lost in the hazy horizon under the grey clouds. The roofs of the buildings on the banks of the Rhine were covered by heavy snow. On the cobblestone streets, carts and the feet of passersby had already hardened and dirtied this layer. It was still extremely cold, and the snow was not showing any signs of melting.

They got off the tram and the two men and the young woman proceeded down to the Ludwigshafen station and while George took Hilda by the arm, Jean picked up her two suitcases and they entered the station. He got a ticket for himself and Hilda and returned to his companions, without showing the anxiety that was praying on his mind, now that danger was threatening again. However, the anguish was lessened a little bit by the idea that George Krahl's uniform probably would protect them without the policeman suspecting a thing.

Suddenly, he noticed that the access to the platform was guarded by policemen. Seeing the control that was put on the travelers, the slim hope that George Krahl's presence would protect him now abandoned him and his courage too. This must surely be the end. He imagined that in a few minutes he would be stopped, they would lead him to a dark, cold prison where he would spend one or two days without even the smallest morsel of food and afterwards, he would be sent back to a prisoner of war camp, or worse yet, maybe, even a concentration camp, given that he was not only a POW, but he had also committed a crime. Ludwigshafen could be the end of his trip and his hope of escape.

A big tremor ran through his whole body as he imagined the fate that awaited him, but even greater than that, he vowed he would not betray the girl who had so kindly rescued him. He would take all the blame, rather than say one word that would raise even the smallest suspicion against her. He would deny the theft of the money, as he no longer was in possession of the proceeds of the involuntary theft. This would bring the investigation to a close and the police would conclude that the owner had simply lost his wallet and one day the man would be returned his property, sent to him anonymously by Hilda Hessling. Then, people like George Krahl would be probing their minds trying to find an explanation for this mystery.

In the meantime, Hilda entertained the young policeman, to ensure that no danger would threaten her traveling companion. Finally, the time of departure was approaching, and she addressed Jean: "Would you please take the suitcases, Heinrich?"

Her air expressed a world of unspoken strategies the fugitive didn't understand, but he did read some encouragement in it. She extended him her hand.

"Please give me the tickets," she said.

He gave them to her, and she gave them to George and said, "Since you're accompanying us to the train, you can do me the pleasure of taking charge of the tickets."

When they were stopped at the security check, George shook hands with one of his colleagues and said a few words to him and the young couple was let on the train without showing any I.D., and they quietly took a seat in an empty compartment without incident. Jean had followed his companions as if he were in a trance, aware that due to George's police status, no one had asked him for his papers. Krahl was there for a reason, no doubt, Hilda had planned and arranged everything, even as far as asking George to accompany them to the station. She had thankfully rescued her friend again.

The policeman did not instantly leave Hilda when the train was about to depart. He shook the girl's hand for a long time, holding it in his and looking into her eyes. When the departure whistle sounded, he gave the fugitive a quick and cordial handshake and left.

67

CHAPTER TWELVE

The same evening, just before sunset, George Krahl went back to visit Hilda's sister-in-law.

"They didn't miss the train?" she questioned, to start the conversation.

"No," answered George, as he removed his gloves and rubbed his hands to warm them up. "Oh! It's so cold! It's also beginning to snow again; tomorrow we'll have a total of at least 20 centimeters."

He extended his hands over the fire and smiled.

"What a girl! She's always in a good mood and always happy."

"It looks as if you've made a declaration of love and she has listened with kindness," observed Martha.

The young man laughed gently.

"She knows how I feel; I don't need to make any declarations. Besides, if I did, I'm pretty sure she'd laugh."

"Don't think that. Do you know that a young woman is always flattered when a man tells her he loves her, even when she doesn't love him?"

"Maybe, but if I tell Hilda that I love her, she probably wouldn't take me seriously. She seldom takes the things that I tell her seriously."

"She's still so young," said Martha, "and when we're young we might as well not be too serious, because later, we don't have the opportunity or the desire to laugh much. But once she becomes Mrs. Krahl, you'll be happy to see her laugh."

"Oh, we're not at that point yet," answered George red-faced; "I've never talked to her about marriage. If I spoke to her about it, she would probably laugh her head off.

"I really wish it were different," said the young man earnestly. "I wish she were a little more serious, that she would talk and think more about the future. It would be sad if all young women were like her. All my friends and colleagues are married and sometimes I'm the object of their taunts because of my single status, but I don't intend to marry any other woman than Hilda."

"She's young," repeated Martha. "You'll see that she will end up wanting your company. She is happy go lucky this time in her life, that's all; but don't think she makes fun of you. On the other hand, I'm certain she is not in love with another man; she would have told me because I'm her confidante and she would have said something."

He didn't answer; he was absorbed in his thoughts. She interpreted his silence as a sign that he doubted her last words and continued: "Here, I found a small address book in the room where she spent the night; she must have forgotten it. If she had a boyfriend, she would certainly have entered a few words to that effect in this datebook, at least, she would have entered his name. It may be a little dishonest on our part to get into Hilda's secrets, but for once, let's not think about the rules of etiquette and do it as an innocent prank."

She turned the pages of the small book looking for a few notes. George stayed facing the fire without turning towards her, as if he wasn't interested.

"There's nothing," Martha said slowly. "Two or three telephone numbers, a friend's address and my husband's address. You can see that I'm right: there is no other man in her life… … but, Ah ha! Wait a minute, here's another address on the back page… and… what a strange name! Stassart, Jean Stassart."

George Krahl whipped around and snatched the little address book out of Martha's hands.

"Here!" he said. "Let me see that!!"

He was so shocked that he fell back into a chair.

"Jean Stassart! And it's a Belgian address! I knew something wasn't right! Now it all makes sense, damn it!" he said in one breath.

"But what's wrong, what have you got?" demanded Martha, alarmed.

The policeman's eyes were flashing, and he shouted.

"And she knew!" he said to himself, ignoring Martha. "I'm positive she knew! She used me to make it simpler for him to escape! Ah! I can't believe she's that cunning!"

His eyes were full of anger and hatred when he looked up at Martha.

"What is going on?" she asked, frightened and not understanding the sudden change in the young man's behavior.

He tried to regain his composure, finding it hard to believe that this sweet, happy go lucky young woman had so totally deceived him.

Addressing Martha, he said, "Your sister-in-law is in enormous danger. The man you were so hospitable to last night, this Heinrich Lutz, or Jean Stassart, is none other than the thief, the escaped prisoner of war from the stalag of Nuremberg that we've been looking for!"

"This young man, so polite, so refined!" said Martha.

"Himself!"

Martha said, "But… and Hilda?"

"Obviously, Hilda said nothing," he uttered in anger, not wanting to admit to Martha his error of being so easily deceived by the young woman he was so fond of. "This individual used her to help him in his escape plan! You understand!" On his way to the door, he yelled, "I hope we can apprehend the rogue this same night!" He immediately dashed out of the house.

CHAPTER THIRTEEN

With extreme joy and relief, Jean saw the buildings and the last of the houses of Ludwigshafen disappear. He was seated across from the young woman just like the previous day. They had found an empty compartment except for one soldier who had entered at the last moment. He hadn't yet started a conversation with his courageous and intelligent companion. He was still too stressed from the peril he had just escaped. He couldn't help admiring her composure under these dangerous circumstances.

The train was already far from Ludwigshafen when the fugitive, being overcome with emotion, found a few words to again express his gratitude. But Hilda enacted the silence with a gesture from her hand.

"Please, I've asked you before, let's not talk about it anymore," she said, "everything has worked out well for the moment and I'm very happy. We haven't finished our trip yet, and who knows what difficulties lie ahead for us on our journey. I'm sure you'll feel more secure in Belgium."

"I hope so, but at least I know I can count on my countrymen. Here, people are only hostile to me."

He took Hilda's small hand in his and added: "Obviously, you're an exception. My personal safety will have increased one hundredfold from the day that money will again be in the hands of the rightful owner."

"It won't be long, I promise you. For now, we need to take care of the rest of our itinerary."

"I couldn't do better than to follow your advice; you know this country better than I do. You'll permit me to take the initiative on the other side of the border."

"Well," she said "We have our tickets to Cologne. At that station we'll buy tickets for Aix-la-Chapelle. I believe it's safer than to request tickets to Belgium. We can't take too many precautions; there's no need to tempt fate. We'll exit the train at Aix-la-Chapelle and my recommendation is to proceed with extreme caution and avoid the police at all costs. When we leave the train at Aix-la-Chapelle, we'll travel to the border on foot, preferably during the night and through fields and forests. After everything we've gone through, it would be horrible to be stopped at the door to your homeland, would it not? Up until now, we have triumphed over all the difficulties, but it's probable that the border will pose greater dangers."

"You always talk in the plural, as if you were being tracked the same as I am," remarked the fugitive.

"It's my assistance," answered Hilda, smiling. "I'm your accomplice now, since I concealed the money and I'm helping a POW."

"In that case, I approve of your plan," he said.

"You are the most honorable woman that I have ever met," he said with emotion. "I will always love you; I only wish this war would end so that we could belong to each other for the rest of our lives."

"See?" she said with a smile, "Good is often born of evil and without this terrible war we would have never known each other."

They remained quiet for a few moments, watching the countryside disappear behind them. The train passed the little village of Frankenthal and continued its course towards the north; in some areas it followed the banks of the Rhine. Soon, the train stopped at the station of the city of Worms.

Hilda continued her role of travel guide just like she did on the trip from Nuremberg to Mannheim, explaining to her companion that Worms was the most ancient city in Germany.

"Thanks to Martin Luther, above all, this city is universally known," she said. "This is where the reformer supported his thesis at the Diet before Charles V."

As they left Worms, the snow again began to fall in thick flakes covering the hills on the banks of the river. Jean never tired of admiring the landscape and he regretted that time and weather conditions kept him from having a sharper and more extended view.

"This must all be very beautiful and scenic in the summer," he murmured. "This time of year, the snow-covered hillsides have a forsaken look to them. In the summer, they must be so beautiful with the green meadows and flowering trees basking in the midday sun."

"In fact," responded Hilda, "the Rhine is the most beautiful river in Germany and without a doubt, one of the most beautiful in Europe. I've followed its course by boat all the way to Dusseldorff. I've always enjoyed seeing its enchanted shores, its cities and its villages, its castles in ruins on the mountains, and the hills covered in vines."

His gaze was lost in the distance where the gray skies mingled with the snowflakes and the white hills.

"Yes, it's beautiful and sad at the same time," and she turned back towards him.

"I just need to tell you one thing," she said, "I'm so happy to have known you and once you get home and you're with your parents and me with mine, when hundreds of kilometers separate us, I'll think of the hours we've spent together and I'll regret that it's over; that this all belongs to the past. I feel joyful in the fact that I've been able to help you; that I was able to do something for you and that you will always remember me. In my mind, I think that what I'm doing for you isn't much, but your eyes tell me that you feel it's something big; heroic even. What other people, my compatriots, think leaves me apathetic, but I value your opinion of me. I truly hope in my heart that you don't have any more hardships, and despite everything that's happened, I will continue to help you during the trip and when you succeed, I will have such happy memories of you. And no matter when circumstances arise that force us to separate, it will be too soon. Later, this whole adventure will seem like a dream; I'll tell myself that it's too fantastic to have lived it and I will continue to relive this memory. But, if one day I receive a letter from you or if I see you again, only then will I realize that it's not a dream, that everything was real, that you exist, and that you are much more than just a figment of my imagination."

Jean listened to his companion with delight; although the frankness with which she explained her feelings troubled him and when she paused, he remained silent. She didn't look at him to see how her words had touched him. Her mind was working, and she changed the conversation.

"Germany has waged war against us, have they not?" she said.

He reddened a little for a moment, thinking about how the German army had crossed the Belgian border and occupied his country and taken all the soldiers to POW camps, and he said, "We are not responsible, not you, not me, for the decisions and the actions of our leaders. I say this, because from the same day your country invaded mine and from the first hour of the war, I have felt hatred against all the people of Germany, with no exception."

He saw that his words were hurting her, but now that he was unburdening his heart from these past months of terror, he couldn't stop himself and he quickly continued. "You don't understand. One must have to have survived what we have lived through; one needs to have seen the misery of my people fleeing the hordes coming from Germany; one needs to have witnessed the dead and wounded, the women and children mutilated by the bombs and shells and so many other unspeakable sights. All we wanted to do was live in peace with the world, but we were a small country and yours has crushed us because of the enormity of your army. If you think about it, you will understand why I hated Germany and all German people. I detested them as much as I love you now. Why would I have killed, without hesitation, the first of your compatriots who would have found themselves in front of the barrel of my gun? As if all the misery that had befallen Belgium was not enough, when we put down our weapons, they herded us by the hundreds of thousands, men, women, and children, to concentration camps and POW camps where we lived like beasts for months, suffering from hunger and the bitter cold. I said that we lived like beasts, but animals were much better off than we were. Animals are fed; they eat until they are satiated. Do you know that there are many among the prisoners whose only desire, is for just one day to eat until their hunger is satisfied? Do you know that the desire to eat kills all other feelings? I trust you've never known hunger. I'll tell you what it is. You fall on food like a wild animal and when your plate is clean, your stomach still complains day after day. You never get enough to eat, and when you finish, you're as hungry as you were when you started eating. You eat grass and leaves off trees; you only think of eating, eating, eating. When you have eaten your daily ration, you try to find another man who has not finished a small morsel of food, you want to jump on him and snatch it up even knowing that he needs it just as much as you do. You would steal and maybe even kill for just a small piece of bread. This goes on for days, weeks, and months. Every night you dream wonderful dreams of being seated at a beautiful table; you find every dish imaginable and eat it. Then, alarm! Despair! When you wake up and realize that it's only a dream. These dreams are not specific to one or another individual; all the men I spoke to talked about the same dreams. One day, another prisoner of war, a farmer, told me that he would be the happiest man alive if he could have the food that he used to feed his pigs and I told him I would eat the same thing with just as much appetite. I have seen hundreds of men waiting for hours in front of a barrack where the guards ate their meals; just in case, by chance one of the guards would throw a small bit of food out a window and the prisoners would pounce on it like a pack of starving dogs. I won't tell you what that miserable little piece of crust looked like by the time it went into the mouth of one of the unfortunates. I exchanged my watch for two loaves of bread, and I felt I made a good deal. Usually, your compatriots only gave one loaf for a watch. If someone had told me that in escaping the stalag I would fall in love with a young German woman, I would have regarded it as an insult."

He saw the beautiful eyes of his friend fixed on him and he understood what pain his words had inflicted on her. Then his bitterness vanished like the darkness before the sun's rising.

"I'm sorry for venting this way," he said. "I promise never to talk about all this again, but it feels good to get my anger out."

In his ire, he had forgotten about the soldier who occupied the other side of the compartment, but he looked over and noticed he was sound asleep and hadn't heard anything.

The train passed the small village of Oppenheim. The snow had stopped falling and Jean stared at the houses situated on a hill under its white coat of snow. Oppenheim had the appearance of a painting on a greeting card. To change the subject, Hilda drew the fugitive's attention to the remains of the fortress of Landskron.

Shortly, they stopped at the Mayence station. Almost two hours had elapsed since their departure from Ludwingshafen.

"We're running late," said the young woman. "I think it must be because of the snow."

Beyond Mayence, the railway track joined the Rhine. Soon they reached Ingelheim and shortly after that, Bingen. Hilda said, "The area between Bingen and Coblenz is the most picturesque of the whole trip through the Vater Rhein region."

The train crossed the Nahe River (a tributary of the Rhine) which flows into the great river at Bingen in the wine region. The Nationaldenkmal monument on the right bank of the Rhine remained invisible because of the snowy fog, but Jean was able to observe the Mauseturm (Mouse Tower) on a rocky island in the river.

On both banks of the river, there were elevations which were crowned by ruins of castles from back in the Middle Ages. However, the visibility was so bad that the opposite shore could barely be seen.

They passed through Bacharach, then Oberwesel. Beyond this last locality, the Rhine suddenly turned to the right between two rock walls. In this area, the river wasn't more than 150 meters wide. At St. Goar, travelers were able to catch a glimpse of the ruins of Rheinfels, which rose at about 115 meters above the Rhine.

At Hirzenach and Bad-Salzig they reached the ancient village of Boppard. Evening was approaching; the sky cleared up and the last rays of sunshine tossed multicolored bursts of light on the imposing Marksburg castle. This fortified castle stood its ground on a rock 150 meters above sea level. Then the train passed Rhens and the Koenigsstuhl rock cliff presented itself to the fugitive and his companion. Hilda told him that this stone structure resembled a pulpit and was originally the meeting place of the electors of the Rhine.

Jean briefly caught sight of the castle of Stolzenfelz but darkness began to fill the valleys and then a few minutes later, when the train stopped at the Coblenz station, nightfall was complete.

CHAPTER FOURTEEN

Jean Stassart was elated when they arrived at Coblenz. The Belgian border was about 100 kilometers from here, as the crow flies; the biggest part of their journey was behind them. All that was left was to travel north to Cologne. Throughout the trip he hadn't felt as if he had gotten close to his goal. Now, after leaving this city, the train was moving directly on its path towards Belgium.

What was really reassuring to him was that in the station of Coblenz there didn't seem to be any sign of guards. *In fact,* he thought to himself, *who could have guessed that he had crossed the distance between Nuremberg and Coblenz so quickly and that no one would think that he had taken this route?* How could he have slipped through the fingers of the police who were guarding the railroad stations all through Bavaria, at Wurtemberg, Baden, and Hesse? Without a doubt, at this moment, he guessed, they were actively searching for him in Mannheim and the surrounding area. Upon leaving the city, he had not left any trace of his passage and he had travelled 100 kilometers further. He had probably gone further than any other prisoner of war who had attempted to escape. He should now have faith in the success of his endeavor, and he could not foresee any other difficulties on the way to the border.

He felt light-hearted and talked happily to Hilda in a cheerful voice. But the stop in Coblenz seemed to take a long time and was beginning to get on his nerves. The young woman also began to look to the left and the right, trying to see if there was anything out of the ordinary happening in the poorly lit station. Their anxiety began to subside when the train finally began to move.

Jean soon realized that the train had significantly reduced speed. He thought at first that the pace would quicken as they left the urban area, but it didn't happen: he attributed this to the heavy snowfall that had occurred during the day and thought no more of it.

Suddenly there was grinding of the brakes along the cars and the convoy came to a halt. The young German put her head under the curtain trying to penetrate the darkness.

"Where are we?"

"I don't know," she said. "There's no station here; the train has stopped in the middle of the countryside."

They read another bout of anxiety in each other's eyes.

"Maybe there's an obstacle on the track," he said. "With all the snow, that can happen."

"Yes, that's possible; it's probably very likely," she answered with some apprehension.

After about 15 minutes, the locomotive resumed her uncertain path, but this time it wasn't for long; the cars moved with a great deal of noise and on multiple tracks and came to a stop at the Andernach station.

It was a new and longer stop during which the passengers opened their windows to try to figure out why the delay. Jean and Hilda fell silent; something was gnawing at them and they became anxious and impatient.

Finally, the young woman expressed the thoughts they both had in their minds: "We will be forced to spend the night in Andernach."

They both thought how dangerous it was to spend the night here. At that time a railroad employee came into the car and announced to the passengers that this train would not be continuing the voyage and that they should find accommodations for the night. There would be a train leaving at 8:00 the next morning for Cologne. People were asking for explanations, but the employee left without giving any details.

"Wait here," said Hilda to her companion, "I'm going to find out what's going on. I'll be back in a couple of minutes."

After a few agonizing moments, the young woman rejoined the fugitive.

"I didn't find out very much except that it's impossible to continue our trip tonight," she said. "Some people are saying that there's been so much snow that the railway traffic has been interrupted; others say that a bridge has been bombed by some British pilots. Regardless, we need to find somewhere to stay for the night."

As Jean watched the last passenger leave the car, he was feeling extremely uneasy. Hilda took him by the arm as she had done several times when she felt emotional.

"Trust me, have no fear, I'll do everything I can to get us out of here," she said nervously.

He saw tears in her eyes, and he understood how deeply she loved him.

"My dear," he said, stroking the curls on her head and hugging her gently against him, forgetting everything for an instant.

"Don't you find it humiliating for a man to lean on a woman and hide behind her skirts?" He said bitterly.

"Let's not waste any time," she interrupted letting go of him.

He took her bags and she put her arm under his; they walked out of the station like a young married couple.

"My dear fiancé," she said with a happy smile.

They entered a hotel called "Laager See" near the station. There were so many travelers in the lobby of the hotel that the young woman was afraid they would not find any available rooms.

"You stay here." he whispered in Hilda's ear. "It's different for me; I have no identity papers. I will need to find another shelter, maybe a hostel."

"Leave it to me," she replied. She returned after several minutes with a radiant face.

"We have a room; I told them to take our baggage up and that we will have our dinner in the room."

He gave her a nod of approval as he looked at their surroundings; he didn't even understand what his friend's intentions were. They followed the employee who was climbing the stairs with the luggage. He led them into a spacious room and set the suitcases down and left.

"Ah! Yes," said Jean, emerging from his thoughts. "So, this is your room."

"It's our room." She said putting an emphasis on the word. Your name isn't on the register, so you can stay here, since no one will know. When they bring our food, you will need to hide so he will know you have already left. I told them you were my brother and that you were staying in another hotel where there was no room for me."

He finally understood what the girl had done, and he took her in his arms and gave her a warm embrace.

"You must love me a great deal to have done all the things you've done. You, a young woman," he said.

"Yes, I do love you a lot," she replied grimly.

They spent the next several minutes embracing and Jean noticed that the hotel employee had neglected to close the curtains. He pulled away to close them and as he approached the window, he suddenly stood still.

"Hilda," he called.

She came over by his side and looked out the window. They had a good view of the station. In the moonlight, the snow was a glittering carpet. They could clearly distinguish everything that wasn't in the shadow of the buildings. Hilda, her eyes wide with astonishment and dismay, noticed several cars arriving at the train station and men in uniform exiting. The cars were situated in front of the buildings of the station and in front of the hotels. The occupants were entering the station, some of them armed with rifles and machine guns.

The young woman fell into the arms of her companion and burst into tears.

"Jean, my poor Jean! You aren't even a criminal. Why are they so desperately against you?"

He also had doubts as to the purpose of this deployment of forces. He sighed deeply. The moment had come to act and his courage grew by the minute before the looming danger that threatened him.

"I'm afraid the time has come for us to part ways," he said. "You have nothing to fear and it's safer that we separate right now before you're involved in this dangerous situation. in my heart I'll anticipate seeing you again someday." He hesitated a moment and then added, "In a few months, perhaps when the war is over. I swear to you I will never forget you and when I see you again, if you will have me, I will ask you to be my wife. Since I won't have the opportunity to take you to my parents now, I just want to tell you something: If I don't return to you, it's because… …"

He didn't finish his sentence nor his thoughts and wanted to leave immediately while he still had the will to go, but she clung to him.

"I won't leave you," she said desperately. "I want to run away with you and share your fate as I've done so far and help you as much as I can. Do you understand what state I'll be in if we separate now? Do you know what mortal anguish I would feel, not knowing where you are and thinking of you being chased like a mad dog who could be shot around any street corner? Jean, my love, if you love me you will let me leave with you."

"But do you know what dangers you could be exposing yourself to?" he asked. His voice displayed painful and delicious emotions at the same time, all caused by his friend's arguments. "If I succeed in escaping again, I would be forced to spend the night outside somewhere in this frigid weather. Do you love me enough to face the dangers and the extreme cold tonight and maybe countless other nights after this?"

She held his embrace so tightly that it was nearly leaving him breathless.

"Yes, my love, I can face anything. It would be more tolerable than the angst I would feel if we parted now."

"My dear Hilda," he said, feeling joyful despite everything that had happened.

"Let us work quickly," she said. "I'll leave my luggage here; it certainly isn't worth a fortune. Let's go!"

They went down to the lobby and Hilda explained to the man at the front desk that they were going across the street to the train station to get some departure information and that they would be back in a few minutes. They left and paused just outside the door to scope out the area. The men who had entered the station had not come back outside; the others were still outside at the corner of the street. Except for the men in uniform, they could see no one else.

The sidewalk across the street from the train station where Jean and Hilda were walking was in complete darkness. On the street, the moon cast a silvery glow on the hard snow, and it was extremely cold.

"We have one chance," the fugitive said quietly. "We'll take one of these cars. We're not really stealing it, because I'll abandon it further down on the road and the owner will regain possession of his property."

A few feet from them, they found a small car, a four passenger. They worked quietly as Jean tried the door and it opened. They swiftly got in, he took a quick glance at the station and satisfied that no one was watching, he pushed down the clutch, put the car in neutral and started it.

The car slid a little on the snow as they drove down the street, while the fugitive kept an eye on the rearview mirror on the armed men behind them on the opposite corner of the street, but they were paying no attention to the car. They continued driving along the wall, sheltered by the icy wind.

As they turned the corner and were out of sight from the guards, Jean stepped on the accelerator and sped straight ahead at full speed. He took another street, barely slowing down in the curves, and then another. He didn't know the city and picked his way haphazardly down each street hoping to reach the countryside as quickly as possible and leave Andernach far behind them.

Soon the houses became sparse, the moon bathing her milky rays on the landscape which was buried under the white coat on the earth. The snow was still soft, since only two or three vehicles had left their mark.

Neither Jean nor Hilda had spoken a single word since they had entered the car. The emotions they felt after taking the car had left them numb and scared without the desire to speak. Hilda opened her purse to find her handkerchief, and as she was searching through it, she softly said to her friend.

"Jean!"

"Yes, dear."

"I don't have my address book."

There was a short silence; he was keeping his eyes on the road as it was speeding under the wheels of the car.

"So, Hilda, did you lose it?"

She thought about it, then: "I must have left it at my sister-in-law's, on the nightstand in the bedroom where I slept," she said.

"Was it very important?"

"I had written your name and address in it."

He didn't answer, he was processing the possible impact of what she had just said to him. Neither one of them said a word… the sound of the tires crunching on the snow seemed very loud. Occasionally, the wind raised a white cloud of the white fluff which would stick to the windshield and make it difficult to see, so Jean activated the wipers. But regardless, little by little, a layer of ice was beginning to form on the windshield. He was only using the parking lights to make it more difficult to see them from a distance.

"And your sister-in-law, what will she do with your address book?"

"She's a woman, so, she'll read everything that's written in it."

"So?" he asked again.

"George Krahl visits her now and then. I'm sure he went over there again after he dropped us off at the train station, later in the afternoon or early evening."

"Do you think she'd show it to him?" he asked.

"I sure hope not, but she'd be really happy if I were to marry him."

Jean stopped the car, got out, and rubbed the windshield to try to get rid of some of the ice that had accumulated because it was almost impossible to see. A very icy wind blew through the car and Hilda shivered and pulled her coat a little tighter. The young man blew on his reddened hands to warm them, and their getaway continued to an unknown destination.

A little further down the road, the fugitives reached a village and Jean turned on his headlights to enable him to see a little better. The rays of light fell on a road sign which read: Nickenich. It was a small village where two roads intersected. He took the road to the left and in a few minutes, after the last of the houses disappeared, Nickenich was left behind.

"I would really like to know where this road leads to," he said.

"I'll be careful to pay attention to the signposts," answered the young woman. "Maybe we'll see a name that one of us may recognize."

The young man was struggling to hold the steering wheel because his hands were aching from the cold. He also knew that it wasn't possible for them to drive all night. They would have to find a place where they could warm up and get some sleep. Sleeping in the car would be impossible; he didn't remember ever being so cold in his life. To make matters worse, the wind was becoming stronger, and making them shiver and he had to fight to keep the car on the road.

A few kilometers past Nickenich, the car went through another village where Hilda read the name: Kruft. The country was becoming quite mountainous and wooded but Hilda didn't give any indication which way they needed to go. The names of the small villages weren't familiar.

They drove through another village called Thur. Travel was still very hazardous, making it difficult to go up some of the slopes and Jean was very careful, especially on the downhills. In certain areas the snow was very thick; so thick that the car would sink up to the bumper, creating a real obstacle. At these times, he had to skillfully maneuver the car and put it in reverse to try to circumvent these areas. The fugitives spoke very little, but their minds were united. Despite their terrible situation and the danger that threatened to come from all sides, being together was a source of solace and happiness. As mutually agreed, the few words spoken were of no relevance to their circumstance - being hunted during the night in the dead of winter.

"Hilda, I love you."

"That makes me so happy, darling."

The young woman's voice was filled with a deep sadness, caused by the eagerness with which her countrymen were pursuing the man she loved. She snuggled against him and he smiled, happy that her friend's body was close to her. This whole strange adventure, good and bad, seemed like a bad dream. If he had woken up and found himself back in the barracks in the stalag in Nuremberg, he would not be at all surprised. Two days had passed since he found himself over there on the hard bed. Now he was driving on unknown roads in the middle of the night, accompanied by a young woman he loved and who loved him.

The first houses of another town appeared: Mayen.

Jean, who was lost in his daydreams, was suddenly shocked back to reality and quickly slowed the car. He saw the silhouettes of two or three soldiers on the road ahead. One of the men was waving a red light, indicating an order to stop. A fleeting thought went through his head of trying to speed up the car and get away from these soldiers. However, just as quickly as the thought crossed his mind, he scrapped it thinking it might be too dangerous and he slowed the car, but when he applied the brake the automobile slid in the snow towards the men. One soldier moved into the middle of the road, while the other two were on the left side of the car with their guns pointed at them.

As he reached the men, Jean made a quick decision, pushed the accelerator to the floor and the car lunged ahead at full speed. The soldier who had taken his place in the center of the road jumped into the ditch at the last moment to keep from being hit by the car. Gunshots rang out and a bullet struck the car. The fugitive seemed to have lost control of the vehicle and it skidded dangerously, zig zagging all over the road: A flat tire!

By reducing his speed, he regained control of the car and no longer zig-zagged, but it kept on skidding. In this manner, he drove through the small town of Mayen, without the slightest concern as to the direction he was going. His only thought was to distance himself from the guards.

Hilda put her arms around her friend's waist, a kind of pity mixed with admiration filled her soul. Here was a man who was defending himself against a whole nation; he had so much courage but was so terribly alone. So weak, compared to his enemy and he had suffered so much. He was a fighter, arms in hand he would have defended the two of them to his last breath.

When he felt her arms go around him, he said simply in a soft voice: "Don't be afraid, darling."

The vehicle climbed a hill with a lot of difficulty and at the top Jean stopped. He turned off the lights, but kept the engine running to be ready for anything that could happen, as he looked for a place to pull off to change the tire.

"I need to change the tire," he said.

"I wish you didn't have to do it," she said sadly.

She began to be apprehensive; she had a premonition that she and her companion were surrounded by guards and that they would have no way to get away. She couldn't help but think about her address book that she had forgotten at her sister-in-law's house and she began to chastise herself for doing such a foolish thing.

Jean began the difficult task of changing the rear tire that had been flattened by the bullet. It was a big struggle; the wind picked up tiny snowflakes that stung his face. Every few moments he was forced to stop working because his stiffened fingers refused to move. He wondered how he was still standing upright, with his feet feeling like blocks of ice. The cold had penetrated his body so much that he was constantly shivering; his teeth were chattering involuntarily. Working in such difficult circumstances made beads of sweat appear on his forehead, which transformed almost immediately into ice. He was breathing heavily and when his hands touched the metal, they felt like they were burning.

The car door opened, and he heard Hilda's voice: "Can I help you with anything, Jean?"

"No," he said with dread, "just close the door quickly to conserve the little bit of warmth inside the car. You can't really be of any help and it's so very cold."

She heard his words, combined with the trembling of his jaw. How he must be suffering… … with a big helpless sigh, she closed the door.

When Jean finally replaced the tire, he had no desire to keep the one he had removed, and he rolled it into the ditch that ran along the road. He returned the tools to the trunk after checking quickly behind him to make sure there were no vehicles on the highway, thankfully, the road was deserted. He sank into the seat of the car, totally exhausted and shaking involuntarily.

Hilda took her friend in her arms and held him against her; she felt such compassion for him.

"My poor dear, you're so cold, however, if we lived in a castle and we were seated by a warm fire, I wouldn't love you more than I do this minute. It's these conditions that double my love for you because it's in times of trouble that you see a person's worth. I hope with all my heart that you will continue to love me once you're far from the danger and misery, which surrounds us right now and I pray that the love for your companion of misfortune will not change when you live a carefree life again."

He had laid his head on his young friend's shoulder and closed his eyes, indulging in the sweet intoxicating embrace. He listened to her gentle chatter while she caressed his face with her little hand. He would have liked to stay this way and fall asleep… … and never wake up again. The trembling began to lessen and eventually disappeared. A delicious peace surrounded him. He had the urge to quit fighting and pay for it with his freedom, so he could spend more time in Hilda's arms, but he rejected temptation and he straightened up.

"Shall we go, dear?"

"Let's go," she said.

Silent tears fell down the young woman's cheeks, but he didn't notice.

The car resumed its course, with the lights out. The moonlight helped illuminate the way well enough and the white countryside slowly slipped behind the fugitives into the past. The land remained mountainous and they rarely saw a house. It was approximately midnight and the road was totally deserted. The noise from the wind howling became stronger and stronger over the noise of the engine and the tires on the snow.

Jean often glanced behind him to be reassured that they weren't being followed. The back window had been shattered by a bullet making it very cold in the car. He checked the odometer and said, "So far, we have travelled about 60 kilometers from Andernach," he noted.

"And I think we are approaching the border of your beloved country," said Hilda. "The area we're crossing must be the Eifel region which flows from Germany across the frontier into Belgium."

Her voice was a bit monotone; you would have thought she was pronouncing these words with regret.

"You're tired," he said. "We need to find a place to stay for the night."

"No," she replied quickly. "We have to continue to drive, all night, if necessary. We have to get to the border as fast as possible."

They drove through two or three more villages until they arrived at a small town. As a precaution, Jean turned on his headlights so as not to arouse suspicion. This locality was situated on the slope of a mountain and bore the name Daun.

Before driving down the streets of the city, Jean glanced behind him again and saw the lights of two vehicles approaching in the distance. He wasn't sure who they were, but he would have preferred that the road would continue to stay deserted. It was necessary to be prepared for all risks, and the presence of two cars heading in the same direction behind them, alarmed him. He took a couple of narrow streets and parked in an obscure place.

"I'm going to walk back to the road where we turned off," he said to Hilda. "I want to see what kind of vehicles these are."

"I'm coming with you," declared the young woman immediately having made up her mind.

When they stepped out of the car, the wind stung their faces and they walked with heads bent forward up to the main road. Before they got there, Hilda stopped her companion.

"Stay here in the shadows of this door. I think it's better that I walk to the main road by myself."

He approved of her decision and she moved forward in the direction of the vehicles, which weren't more than 100 meters away. The cars were about Hilda's height and they were about the size of the vehicle they had taken.

A terrible fear overcame Hilda when the cars stopped so near her. Nevertheless, she ignored them and continued to walk, looking straight ahead.

A police officer stepped out of the back of the first vehicle and immediately walked with quick steps in the direction of the girl. She didn't stop; she could feel her heart beat all the way up into her throat. The policeman walked in front of her, saluted politely, and asked: "Miss, have you seen a car on the road, a vehicle which looks much like ours?"

"Yes, sir."

"How long has it been?"

"I saw it when I left my sister-in-law's house about fifteen minute ago."

"Thank you very much."

The officer walked back to the car and the two vehicles left. For a few minutes, Hilda continued to walk in the same direction and as soon as the vehicles disappeared, she turned and walked back to her friend.

CHAPTER FIFTEEN

In the first of the two vehicles was George Krahl, in deep thought; when the officer who had questioned Hilda got back into the car, he said, "You should have asked the young lady for her identification."

"What good would that have done?" responded the officer, shrugging his shoulders.

"You never know. It surprises me that a young woman would be walking alone after midnight in this Siberian cold."

"This is not what we should be preoccupied with right now; we have another more important mission to complete," said the officer, dryly. "It's a man we're seeking, not a girl, or, a girl and a man."

But Krahl was concerned with another issue that lay heavily on his mind.

"Her mannerisms, the way she stood," he said almost to himself. "I could be wrong because it is pitch black and yet … … the hat, the coat … … but no, it's impossible. Why would they have stopped here, unless … … … a car failure!!!"

He bolted upright.

"Damn!" he cried. "Without a doubt, it must have been her! They're here, in Daun!"

George cursed again and told the driver to stop. He got out of the car and walked back to the second vehicle and ordered them to continue to Gerolstein and wait for them at the entrance to the city.

The car, occupied by Krahl, turned around and rushed at full speed to the Daun police station. The officer and Krahl hurried into the station, barking brief and clear orders. Policemen were to immediately sweep the streets of the town searching every hotel, hostel, and establishment that provided lodging. All outsiders, male and female, were to be taken to the police station to verify their identity. Agents were to accompany each officer in his car to monitor the roads. Eventually, at this late hour, they would be able to follow the tire tracks leading out of town.

About an hour after Jean and Hilda left Daun, George Krahl and his superior were directing their car down the same road. George was wondering what approach to take regarding the girl he had once loved when he apprehended her.

CHAPTER SIXTEEN

The road on which Jean Stassart drove the vehicle was very narrow; no other vehicles had left a trace in the snow, which had been falling heavily in the area. The wheels of the vehicle sank deeply in the snow, preventing him from driving very fast. Furthermore, he had to drive with caution. The road was very dangerous with steep hills and sudden curves.

The wind was continually blowing with the same violence as before and large clouds were beginning to appear and would soon cover up the moon, making it difficult to see without turning on his headlights.

Jean turned on the headlights again and at times, he was forced to get out of the car and take the ice off the windshield wipers, which would not remove the snow from the glass because the accumulation of snow blown by the storm was sticking and made visibly almost impossible. It was a laborious task, but he was doing it without a word of complaint.

The fugitives did little talking; they were shivering and numb with cold as they watched the white mass fleeing under the vehicle. Hilda slid over next to her companion and again put her arm around his waist. At times she would say his name to prove her love for him and to bolster his courage. At these times he felt happy despite everything that was happening; he repeated her name with a voice full of tenderness.

Once when he got back in the car after having cleared the windshield of ice, she put her arms around his neck and for an instant, he tasted the delicious embrace of a woman who loved him. He hugged her closely and sighed. As he did so, very close to his ear, he heard the ticking of Hilda's watch counting down the seconds to eternity, and this subtle noise brought him back to reality.

"How noble and generous you are," he said. "You deserve every joy in the world and I would love to spend the rest of my life making your life as happy and fulfilling as I can." She remembered him saying these words before, and that she had been so happy at those moments.

He straightened and started the car back up.

"I don't think we're very far from the border, we'll probably get there before morning," she said. "What are we going to do with the car?"

"We'll hide it in the woods," he answered.

"If it's not discovered for two or three days that will be great as we'll already be safely in Belgium and if they discover it in the area where we cross the border, it won't really matter."

A few hundred meters further, they passed through a small village, then a few kilometers more, another one. Jean was taking random roads, absolutely ignoring the countryside. All he knew was that he was somewhere between the Rhine River and the Belgian border, and assumed he was driving in a westerly direction. He kept hoping they would encounter a signpost that would tell his young friend where they were.

An hour had gone by since they had left Daun. It began to snow again, first a few flakes, then increasing to a curtain which was impenetrable by his headlights. The wind chased the snowflakes in all directions, sweeping in from the fields and accumulating the snow in hollows and valleys. Whole packets of white flakes were tossed off the trees and against the windows. With the tires and body of the car moving everywhere, there was no resistance, hindering the operation of the windshield wipers and making the vehicle have the appearance of a ghost merging with the whiteness of the land. The voices of the storm dominated all other sounds, screaming at very high elevations and causing a mournful whistling in the bare branches of the trees, beating with a loud uproar on the surface of the earth.

Neither Jean nor Hilda said a word. They were both watching nature with awe and respect as it unleashed the storm with an irritated voice. Jean had again slowed the speed of the vehicle; they were traveling almost at a snail's pace to try to stay in the middle of the road.

Several times he needed to get out of the car to remove the snow which had piled on the windshield, sinking up to his knees and dipping his icy feet in the white matter. Despite the precautions he was taking, each time he opened the door a burst of wind would throw snow into the vehicle. He had become almost immune to the physical suffering and severe pain, and only uttered a small groan when the windshield wiper tore some skin off the palm of his hand.

Hilda could feel the fugitive's pain in her heart. First, he had fought and overcome so many obstacles and was continually renewed each time with great courage; then, little by little, he began to do move instinctively and automatically like a robot. Eventually, the manner how he got in and out of the car, was no longer the same. He put his feet in the snow almost like a sleepwalker; he didn't even react when his hands touched an extremely cold object on the outside of the car, however, she was pleased to see that this state of insensibility left when he felt his body against hers. Then, his eyes, focusing with a total lack of expression on the blanket of snow that the head-lights were trying to pierce, brought some tenderness to her heart and made her want him to stop the car so she could jump into his arms.

The escapees had just driven through a village, 2 or 3 kilometers back, when a human form appeared in the snow in front of the car; for a moment an arm rose but then the silhouette sank into the thick snow which covered the road. Since the snow-storm had not decreased in intensity, the car was only a few meters away when they noticed the person and the fugitive stopped immediately in front of the outline on the road. Jean and Hilda looked at each other in the semi-darkness.

Without saying a word, the prisoner got out of the car again. Her eyes followed his form, beaten by the wind and advancing slowly. He picked up a young boy and brought him into the car.

It was a child of about 10 years of age; his face had a bluish tint to it and big tears of thin ice lay on his cheeks. He looked at the fugitive with pleading, fearful eyes.

Jean took off his overcoat and wrapped it around the body of the small boy and began to rub him all over to try to warm him; next he removed his shoes and put his scarf around his feet to slowly warm them up to aid in preventing frostbite. After a few minutes, when his feet felt warmer, he dried them with the overcoat and put the shoes back on the boy's feet. Then the boy sat up in the seat and looked at Hilda and Jean with a mixture of confidence and fear.

The fugitives, in questioning the child, learned how he found himself on this iso-lated road in the middle of the night. His father was very strict and after being dis-obedient, made him leave the house. He walked until evening when he found a gamekeeper's cabin in the woods and went inside. After a couple of hours, he got scared and left the cabin and again began to walk without daring to enter another house. In the end he got tired and exhausted, and lay down on the road, and when he saw the approaching car, he raised his hand.

First, Jean and Hilda learned that he lived in Prum; this village wasn't familiar to them and the child could give them no information about the area, or which direction to take. Second, the boy had a terrible fear of his father and begged the fugitive not to take him home. Jean talked to him in a tender voice, telling him that he would talk to his father and assuring him his father wouldn't do him any harm. In the meantime, Jean started the car back up and they continued down the road.

Hilda had been watching this scene unfold between the child and her friend with astonishment. Jean was so gentle with the boy and taking care of him seemed to have made him forget that he himself was being vigorously pursued, and that he could pay for it with his freedom at any time by providing care to this lost child. Even the ultimate success of his plan could be compromised by his act of compassion towards the son of a man he didn't know and whom he considered one of his enemies. He could easily have just simply left the boy in the car and locked it when he abandoned it and went on his way without losing precious time. If the boy had survived and had been picked up by the police, he could have eventually told his story when they were long gone.

They reached a crossroad; a signpost indicated the road toward Prum. Jean took this road and soon they were driving on the roads of this small town. The boy pointed out the house where his parents lived, and Jean stopped the car in front of it.

He barely needed to knock; the door opened at once and a man stood in the doorway and asked him if he was there regarding his son. The prisoner of war answered in the affirmative and added: "Your son seems to be very afraid of you; I beg you to treat him gently. We found him lying on the road quite a long way from here."

Hilda was waiting in the car with the boy in her arms. The man saw them in the half light and invited them inside. Hilda carried him out of the car and the boy went inside and the man took him in his arms and hugged him. Jean checked the expression on Hilda's face to see if they should accept or decline the invitation to enter the house. His friend gave him no sign so after a moment's hesitation, he accepted. Meanwhile, the man yelled inside: "Rosa? Wilfried has been found!"

Somewhere from inside the house a door opened, casting a bright light in the corridor where Jean and Hilda stood. Then everything was plunged back into obscurity when Wilfried's father closed the door that accessed the street. For a few seconds there was a profound silence, interrupted only by the whistling sound of slippers approaching. Jean began to think maybe entering the house wasn't such a good idea and was overcome by a strange foreboding; he focused on two things-- this unfamiliar house and the abandoned car outside. A small voice that was no longer of this world, but that of his grandmother who had died six years earlier, whispered in his ear the words that he had heard hundreds of times when he was a child: "Be careful, my little one."

Then the troubling silence was broken by the voice of the man who growled: "Rosa, why did you close the door? It's very dark in here."

Jean could hear him groping in his pocket, and then the sound of a match striking a box and a flickering flame illuminating the shape of a woman who now stood close to them.

She looked at the man and the fugitive detected what he thought was fear in her eyes. She quietly stammered a few words to her husband which Jean couldn't make out and she took the boy from the father's arms. By the light of the match, the fugitives followed the woman. Jean was still regretting having entered this house, but he also thought that Hilda needed to warm herself and maybe they would be able to get something to drink and perhaps even something to eat.

The man of the house led them to a rustic living room with old furniture. A delicious fire was burning in the fireplace and an agreeable temperature reigned in the room. Three men were seated in the chairs around the table and several cigarette butts filled three or four ash trays. The presence of the three men seemed odd to Jean, both due to the late hour and he hadn't noticed a car outside.

The prisoner of war didn't even hear the woman thanking him for bringing her boy back. He left it up to Hilda to explain under what circumstances the young boy had been found; he continued to watch the three men, looking from one to the other trying to determine whether they were friends or enemies. His scrutiny didn't tell him anything; the trio were in civilian clothes with no indication as to their social status. They probably weren't peasants, but he couldn't tell whether they were industrialists, traders, or officials. And this is precisely what he needed to figure out. They were all about his age, between thirty-five to forty years old.

They listened intently as Wilfried's father retold the story that Hilda had told while looking alternately at the young woman and the young man. When he was finished, the father shook Jean's hand and thanked him for everything he had done for his son. Then, the three men took their turn in shaking Jean's hand one by one. The last man addressing Jean, said: "You don't need to worry about the state of your clothes and your shoes. The young lady told us about what you've gone through, it's no wonder you're soaked from your feet up to your knees."

He smiled and his two companions did the same. Jean felt uneasy, sensing that they were scrutinizing him. If he was wrong, he wondered what the connection could be between them and their host.

Then the trio went to pay their respects to Hilda. Each of them had a few words to say to her while pretty much ignoring him. The anxiety he felt in the hallway hadn't left him. If he was really in danger, he truly had no idea. He found it odd to be in this room, in the middle of nowhere, at this late hour and in the presence of three strangers. Meanwhile, a discussion started among the master of the house, the three men, and Jean's companion. As always, when he was in the presence of other Germans, the fugitive merely said essential words while Hilda did most of the talking to avoid Jean being perceived as a stranger.

Wilfried had seated himself close to the fire and was no longer moving, wishing no doubt, not to attract his father's attention. The child's mother was cutting some bread and preparing coffee. The prisoner of war, occupied by other thoughts, kept losing the sense of the conversation and did not know what anyone was talking about, until one of the men addressed him directly: "What made you decide to pass through here to go to Aix-la-Chapelle travelling from Coblenz?"

"I got lost; it's the first time I have travelled this way," answered Jean.

"Obviously," said the other, with what seemed to Jean a slight bit of mockery in his voice. "Do you live in Aix-la-Chapelle?"

"Yes."

"My brother lives there too. What street do you live on?"

The young man had never been there, and the question caught him off guard; he froze in terror. However, he had a quick mind and from his history lessons, he remembered that Charlemagne is closely linked with this area and all its events, so he took a chance and promptly said: "On Charlemagne Street."

Jean didn't even know if this street really existed. Thankfully, the hostess began serving coffee and invited both he and Hilda to sit at the table and have something to eat.

The gratitude Jean felt toward the woman was twofold. It ended the conversation and it eased the hunger that tore at his stomach.

For the first time, he began to pay attention to the conversation the men were having with his companion, referring to her youth and beauty. Some of their comments were not without a double meaning. She laughed insensitively and he couldn't help but feel a pang of jealousy. He determined they should plan to leave this house as soon as possible.

As soon as they had finished eating, one of the three men rose, and his two companions immediately did the same. Noticing their eyes were fixed on him, Jean felt danger in this gesture and stood up in turn. The three men looked at the master of the house and seemed to hesitate a moment. "So," the first man addressed the prisoner of war, "I suppose you have all the necessary papers proving your identity? We don't doubt your honesty for a moment, but our orders are very precise. We're convinced, on the other hand, that we have the honor to be in the company of a very important man who has a critical place in the German community and the party. The proof is in the journey you're making by car. We believe, therefore, that you are responsible for an important mission and I apologize, that this forces us to fulfill our duty to you."

A deafening silence, like one that comes before a storm, fell over the room after these words, which were expressed in extreme courtesy, but which the fugitive believed were in the same sarcastic tone the man had used earlier.

All eyes were riveted on him, even those of little Wilfried who, without understanding what they were saying to the man who had rescued him, felt there was something unpleasant or threatening directed towards him. Hilda came over to stand next to her friend and wondered how to deal with the imminent peril that was lurking. Her mind was clinging franticly to the idea of buying a little time, a few minutes, even a few seconds.

They saw a smile appear on the man's face and plunging his hands deep in his pockets presenting a casual air, he said: "A person who is taking a trip of several hundred kilometers in the middle of the night, without I.D. papers, in a country that is involved in a war, would certainly be one of the biggest idiots."

"Without a doubt," Jean hastened to reply.

"Also, that we are obliged to ask you for your papers is only a formality."

At that moment, the boy's mother intervened and after giving her husband a timid glance, asked if she had permission to speak.

"This man has saved our child," she said. "He is obviously an honest, caring man. So, why all this red tape?" The woman seemed very anxious. Maybe her instinct warned her that something wasn't quite right with this stranger who had given her back her son. The child, who was sitting so still, came over to stand beside her. The man who had done all the talking turned toward the child's father and said: "I understand all the gratitude you feel towards this gentleman, but please understand that we must do our duty."

This time it was Jean, himself, who intervened. "Gentlemen," he said, "it's not my intention to avoid the process, which I fully understand."

Then, addressing Hilda with an intense plea, he continued, "Hilda, would you please go find my papers in the car? They should be either above the sun visor or in the glove compartment."

"Yes," she said, "I'll get them."

She left the room hesitantly, not fully understanding what her friend wanted her to do but thinking that he must have a good reason for sending her out to the car. The prisoner of war watched her leave, hoping frantically that she had understood his hidden meaning.

"I have been delegated by the establishment Kroll of Nuremberg," he lied to the others. "I've been sent to Coblenz by the Wehrmacht with an important delivery. My mission is no secret and my papers will help convince you."

The tension in the room seemed to subside a little with the soft assurances from the fugitive. When he realized the importance of the man he faced, one of the three men said: "I hope you'll excuse our conduct. Trust that this situation is pretty unpleasant for us after what you have done for our colleague."

"Please don't give it another thought," Jean replied, no less politely than his interrogator. "You're just doing your job. During these times of war, each of us has duties or missions to perform that we don't like, but it's all part of the job."

He turned toward the door through which the young woman had disappeared earlier: "But why is she taking so long? Those papers shouldn't be that hard to find."

He opened the door and yelled: "Hilda, can't you find them?"

Without waiting for a reply, he darted out the door and slammed it behind him. He jumped in the car, started it, put it in gear, floored it, and loudly sped away.

The young woman wasn't too surprised about what was happening. She had trusted that her friend had been planning some sort of stunt. She had understood that he wanted her to get in the car and she had obeyed and waited for what would develop.

While the vehicle was leaving the village of Prum at top speed, the fugitive thought that the end of his adventure was getting close. He knew that this locality wasn't very far from the Belgian frontier and the next few hours would determine his escape or defeat. Yet he didn't know the area and was driving randomly on whichever roads presented itself, propelled only by the need to put a lot of distance between them and the town they had just left.

The roads led them into wooded mountains and the wind continued its angry voice, roaring as loudly as a rolling assault from a tank.

The snow had stopped falling but the wind was picking up the snow and throwing it in all directions so that the fugitive was forced again to continually stop and wipe the windshield.

He was overcome by extreme exhaustion and an urgent need to sleep engulfed him, however, he continued his course, without headlights, with his eyes fixed on the unknown landscape. His eyes began to close, and it was a constant fight to stay awake.

Finally, he abandoned the main thoroughfare and turned onto a small road which went into the woods. He drove a short distance and stopped the car.

"It's probably not wise to stop here," he said. "We're still only a few dozen kilometers from Prum but I don't think we're in any immediate danger."

When the girl didn't answer, he continued wearily.

"I have no idea what direction I should take, so it's useless to continue. I think it would be better to wait here until dawn and get some sleep."

"Yes, sleep a little," said Hilda sounding discouraged, causing the fugitive's heart to ache for her.

Fatigue had plunged the young woman into a strange indifference to everything that was going on around her; the need to sleep had taken over her whole body. Absolute rest during the early hours was essential to calm his nerves and was vital to both their salvation. He needed for his thoughts to be lucid and he had to be in control of all his faculties to begin the last phase of their escape.

Jean's head slid gently onto the cushions until he reached his friend's shoulder and he closed his eyes. He covered them up as much as possible with their clothes to preserve the heat from the excessive cold that was beginning to penetrate the car when he shut down the engine.

He listened to his companion's regular breathing for a few minutes while she was dozing. She surrounded him with her arms, and he laid his cheek against hers. Then, exhausted by fatigue and the emotions of the day, he fell asleep.

CHAPTER SEVENTEEN

Day dawned, enveloped in a thick, grey fog. The fugitive woke up and felt very cold and almost at the same time, the young woman opened her eyes. She involuntarily pushed against him and he hugged her to his heart.

"This is how I want to wake up every morning," she said, surrendering to his embrace.

After a few minutes, she added: "Now, we need to cross the border as quickly as possible. We may not be too far away."

He looked at her, in desperation.

"In which direction do we need to go?" he said. "We can't see anything past ten paces ahead of us because of this fog. I'm been wondering if we should abandon the car now."

He glanced outside at the curtain of fog and at the road.

"The snow is so thick," he said thoughtfully.

He felt his indecision begin to win and he was frustrated. Action was needed to complete this task, which so far had succeeded. Despite all the obstacles they had endured, he had to rebuild his energy and his courage.

"We have nothing to eat," he said again and trying to sound positive, he said, "but I hope that in Belgium we'll find everything we need."

She would have liked for him to sound more confident and she felt saddened. She raised her head and responded: "These are details we don't need to focus on right now. It seems to me that the fog is slowly beginning to lift."

"So," he said, "I need to try to orient myself. If I take a westerly direction, we should arrive in Belgium, there's no doubt about that. I'll see if the gas tank has enough fuel to make it a few more kilometers, because it's possible that we still have some distance to go before reaching the border. I think that we could possibly get there around two or three o'clock."

He straightened up and, wrapping his overcoat around him, got out of the car. The wind had diminished and there was complete silence in the woods. The fog was dissipating little by little and an enchanted landscape met the fugitive's eyes. Everything was immaculately white; not one footprint had soiled the white carpet. The tops of the pines were slightly bent over under the snow's weight. The smaller branches were decorated with a crystal band of frost. As the fog disappeared, the painting became more extended and more grandiose. Soon, other hills and woods appeared and, from the top of the hill where the fugitive found himself, he could see a path down and up again which got lost behind the next hill. The sun at first was a pale red disc, and became brighter little by little, throwing a blinding brilliance over the landscape.

Jean broke a branch off a bush, removed the cap from the gas tank, and measured how much gas was remaining in the tank. The tank was almost empty. He put the cap back on and carefully studied the trees which formed a hedge along the path. Then he returned to the vehicle and got in.

"The Belgian border must be in this direction," he said to Hilda, pointing towards the left. "The prevailing winds are from the west and the tilt of the trees is towards the east, so, we need to go in the opposite direction. There isn't much gas left so, we'll continue to drive on these small deserted roads until it runs out of gas, then we will abandon it and walk the rest of the way."

He pressed the start button and the engine, having cooled, took a few tries but eventually started. In a cheerful voice he said: "We're off on our last lap."

What was indecision a few minutes ago, gave way to courage and resolution. He drove the car slowly down the path. The tires sank almost entirely in the snow, and the mud presented a serious obstacle. The car continued to roll down the road and the fugitive didn't need to force it to go downhill.

At the bottom of the hill, they came upon a larger road. The fog persisted in this valley but was declining rapidly. Determined, Jean turned to the left and increased his pace. A few vehicles had already traveled this road and the snow wasn't too thick or too soft.

In addition to that, his confidence was growing. They were nearing the end of the trip and at least the greatest difficulties and dangers were behind them. The road was almost deserted; there were few houses and he had not seen any official vehicles. If this road led to Belgium, as he thought, they would probably get there near daybreak.

"Hilda," he said, "we need to ask someone if we are going in the right direction and how many kilometers it is to the border. A few kilometers from there we will abandon the car somewhere where it will sit unnoticed for at least several hours. Then, we'll go on foot through the woods. I only hope it won't be too strenuous for you."

"Don't worry about me," she replied. "Once we're out of danger and walking, I'm sure I won't feel so fatigued anymore."

He let go of the steering wheel for a moment to give her hand a squeeze, and a smile of happiness appeared on his face. A sweet feeling of hope made his heart soar.

He stopped the car in front of a small farm situated along the road.

"Maybe we should try to get some directions here," he said.

"Yes," she agreed.

She got out of the car and ran towards the farmhouse as he followed her with his eyes, his look caressing her elegant silhouette. After about five or six minutes, she returned.

"This road actually leads to Belgium," she announced. "We're only about 10 kilometers from the border."

The fugitive sprang from his seat and grabbed Hilda in his arms.

"That's great news, darling! We are almost at the end of our worries!"

After this manifestation of joy, he started the car back up. For a couple of kilometers, the trip went on with no incidents and the border was getting closer. If the people at the farm had given exact directions, about 10,000 meters separated the fugitives from Belgium.

"We'll take the first road across the border and we'll hide the vehicle in the woods," said Jean, happily.

They reached the top of a high hill and what he saw made the prisoner of war realize that he had made a big mistake; perhaps a fatal mistake: the awareness that he should have abandoned the vehicle much sooner. His concern to conserve his friend's strength had led him to wait to find a hiding place for the car until the last moment. He became conscious of his error when, 200 meters ahead, he could see several soldiers guarding the road.

The fugitive felt his heart sink. The soldiers had without a doubt seen the vehicle. To turn around at this point would raise their suspicions and they would be pursued immediately. A short distance away, he noticed a crossroad leading into the woods up the hill and his heart soared. He drove the car onto this road but at the same time, a noise in the engine announced that the fuel was getting very low. The car took a few leaps, shaking up the carburetor, which fed it a few more drops of gas, and the engine turned over again. The car began to climb the slope of the hill.

Meanwhile, the young woman, casting a side glance at the guards, saw two men driving up the road they had just left.

After a few meters, the engine stopped. Jean got out and gave the car a few violent shakes. In doing so, the little gasoline that was left in the bottom of the reservoir fed the carburetor and he was again able to start the engine. The car proceeded, but in the meantime, the two soldiers had reached the road. Noticing the vehicle was having trouble; they quickened their course.

The car rolled for 10 or so meters and then with a loud noise began to shake. The fugitive glanced uneasily in his rearview mirror; the pursuers were gaining ground.

"If we can reach the top of this hill, we would be saved," he said. "We don't need gas to go down the other side and we could possibly get a good lead."

The soldiers probably understood this too, because Jean and Hilda heard a bullet hit the back of the car.

"They're shooting at us!" cried Hilda in terror.

Jean didn't respond. Tight lipped, he pressed down on the accelerator and pushed forward. A few meters still separated them from the summit of the hill, which he saw as the promised land. As the car jerked forward a few meters, they reached the highest point and rolled down the other side, gently at first but increasing in speed as it went down.

The soldiers arrived at the top of the hill and, seeing their prey escape, shot several times at the fugitives. Bullets were striking the car and dangerous whistling could be heard from the gunshots. The vehicle suddenly leaned to the left and Jean had all the trouble in the world driving through the piles of snow which covered the way.

"We have a flat tire!" he yelled.

Hilda didn't respond; she looked at her friend in intense pain and a loud moan escaped her contorted mouth. A bend in the road made the car escape the soldier's sight. It was time, the car was no longer obeying the fugitive's hands and went crashing into a tree.

"Quick, run into the woods," said Jean. "We are near the frontier and we'll rest at the first Belgian farm we see."

He got out of the car and the young girl did the same but with a painful effort that Jean didn't notice in his haste to get away. She took a few steps, fell, rose to her feet, and fell again. In three steps he was by her side, his heart feeling great compassion.

"You're totally exhausted, my poor friend," he said.

He picked her up in his arms and walked with difficulty into the woods. Soon his strength betrayed him, and he was forced to lay her down in the snow. Only then did he see the mortal pallor on his companion's face.

"Continue alone; leave me here," she said, with labored breathing. "They can't do me any more harm."

The meaning of her words escaped the fugitive and he was seized with horror as he saw the blood stains in the snow and on the young woman's clothes. She must have taken a bullet from one of the soldiers during the chase but, he was convinced that it wasn't too serious. In his mind he wasn't willing to admit for an instant that she had a fatal wound. She had rescued him with an inspiring devotion, leaving all the comforts of a normal trip, to travel the road of chance and danger and face a Siberian frost.

Surely death couldn't be the reward for such noble actions. He must talk to her, reassure her, and convince her that her wound wasn't serious.

"Listen to me, Hilda," he said. "It's useless to continue to struggle any longer. In a moment our pursuers will be here, and I will be arrested, but that's no longer of any importance now. You need to be treated and you'll recover quickly. You're not seriously hurt, and in a few days, you will be well again. As for me, when I'm a free man again I'll come and see you in Nuremberg or in Manheim at your sister-in-law's."

It had been only a few minutes since he laid her down and already the snow was saturated with blood. He realized in wild horror that, undoubtedly, she hadn't heard anything he had said.

"You love me, don't you?" She asked, in a very feeble voice, like a breath that had no strength to speak.

He looked fretfully through his pockets for a handkerchief. He raised his friend's head with caution and let her rest it in the crook of his arm as he pressed the handkerchief to the wound in her back, where her life was fading away. He understood that her lungs were damaged, and tears streamed profusely down his face. He felt neither the cold nor the dampness of the snow, and wild despair overtook him.

"Hilda, Hilda!" he cried. "I'll take care of you; I'll bandage your injuries. Yes, I love you! I adore you and that's why you MUST live, do you understand? You have to live for yourself and for me."

She fixed her eyes on his and answered very gently: "I'm happy, I will live."

He saw her gaze begin to fade and he lowered his cheek until his lips brushed her mouth. In one breath he heard again the words: "Liebling." Then her head bowed slightly, and her eyelids slowly closed. She wasn't moving any longer. He realized that it was over, but it was impossible to measure the whole meaning of this tragedy. Everything had happened so terribly quickly. In only a few minutes this young girl, full of life, was transformed to a corpse, bloody and lifeless. He slowly became aware of the fact that this stranger had made the extraordinary sacrifice of her youth, and her life, for him.

He held her head, so loved, against him to try to calm his wrenching pain, and he felt a bitter remorse for his responsibility in all that was happening. If he hadn't used this sweet young person to accomplish his purposes, this wouldn't have happened, and Hilda Hessling would still be alive. Ah! If only he could take back these last two horrific days.

How long he sat there in the snow, seeing nothing but the dead body of the young woman stretched out before him, he didn't know. Life had stopped; he was insensitive to physical pain. Gradually his mind became void of all thoughts and he felt as if his heart had turned to stone. All his memories left him: his escape, his country, and his parents. They no longer existed. He was living a horrendous nightmare and soon he would wake up again in the camp of the prisoners of war in Nuremberg. It wouldn't even matter to him if he had a future or if he never breathed another breath. What he had lived through in the last few days, since he met this young girl, was just an insignificant moment, until now, when everything was too unbelievable to be real. Nobody should have to go through what he and Hilda had gone through. He should have been arrested sooner, then this wonderful girl would still be alive. Yes, it was a nightmare, and when he woke up, he would be relieved not to have been the direct cause of death of this young girl, so kind and gentle.

Soon, two vehicles came rushing up the hill and stopped near his car. Several men got out and followed the fugitive's footprints in the snow until they reached him. He didn't notice them, or even care that they were pointing their guns at him. They encircled him in silence, watching with curiosity and with respect, the bloody table before them. Then a man exited the last car and crossed the circle that had formed around Jean and Hilda's lifeless body. The man, becoming almost as pale as the corpse, fell to his knees by the young girl.

Jean recognized George Krahl and his presence brought him back to reality. He saw George's pain, the intense pain he felt about this tragic event. But Jean's own agony left him indifferent to what George was feeling.

"My God, how did this happen?" demanded George.

The fugitive stared at him with cold, unseeing eyes and didn't reply. George attempted to put his arm under Hilda's body to pick her up, but Jean knocked it away and pushed him aside.

"Who killed her?" demanded the policeman.

The prisoner of war continued to give him a cold vicious stare and George stood up. Jean did the same, then he confronted the policeman and slowly he jabbed his finger into the disgusting Nazi sign in front of him, the swastika underneath the eagle's outstretched wings that George wore on his uniform, and said: "This is what killed her. This symbol of hatred and evil!"

They faced each other, one man with an arrogant air, having a whole country and an army to back him, and the other having only the lifeless body of a young girl on his side. Two adversaries, two rivals, and two nations. Jean's lips pursed with contempt and he spat at George, defying the policeman despite his powerlessness. But George, forgetting his mission and his profession for a moment, only wished to prove that there was a heart beating underneath his uniform.

"My God," he repeated, addressing the prisoner, "how I regret all this. My God, how I regret it."

There were tears in George's voice, but Jean felt not one ounce of pity for the man.

"You will never feel as much remorse as I do," Jean said in a hostile tone.

Then, George Krahl, his Nazi training kicking back in, suppressing all his emotions, turned to the men who were watching in astonishment, and said in a harsh voice, "Take this man to the car and two of you stay with him at all times. Afterwards, we will make arrangements for the … … … … for the body to be removed."

As he was shoved into the police car to be returned to Nuremberg, the last vision Jean Stassart took with him in his heart and his conscience, as he stared out the window of the car was the pale face of his companion through this devastating tragedy, blending with the whiteness of the snow.

ACKNOWLEDGEMENTS

Thanks to my father, Firmin, for giving me the opportunity to translate his manuscript. I thoroughly enjoyed this task, as it took me back to my roots and childhood in Belgium and reacquainted me with French, a language skill I was slowly losing. Thanks to both my parents for having had the courage to sell most of their belongings in 1951 and move our family from Belgium to Canada. The Korean war began in 1950 and my father believed that it would escalate into another world war. He wished to shield his young daughters from ever experiencing the two world wars that he and my mother lived through and Canada seemed the safest place to immigrate. Looking down from heaven, I'm sure he is very proud that his manuscript has now been translated into English after all these years.

Thanks to my son, Eric, for creating the cover for his grandfather's book.

I would also like to thank my friend, Colleen Leyva, who one afternoon when I sat wondering who I could get to edit this book, said "Hello, I'm a teacher, I could edit your book."

ABOUT THE AUTHOR

Firmin Maertens was born in Izegem, Belgium, in 1910. He died in St. Thomas, Ontario, Canada, in the year 1999. He was drafted into the Belgian army in 1939. In May 1940, the Germans invaded Belgium. The Belgian army surrendered by order of Leopold III, and the Germans occupied the country until 1945. Firmin, along with other Belgian soldiers who were still in uniform after the surrender, was detained by the Germans and taken by train to a POW camp in Nuremberg, Germany. The stalag included Belgian, French, and English POWs. On June 6, 1940, Germany made the decision to release all Flemish speaking Belgians in the camps *(reason unknown) and began returning them to Belgium. Firmin (Flemish speaking) was released from Stalag XIIIA on July 10, 1940. After his release and return to Belgium, and being bilingual, he wrote this book in French. Although this is a book of fiction, his brief portrayals of some of the hardships of life in the stalag and his dreams of escape during his captivity are accurate. It's my belief that in writing this book and growing up and having had many conversations with him about the atrocities of war, was therapeutic for him. He never forgot the war or the suffering he and my mother endured. When he retired, he gave me this manuscript to translate into English and I began to work on it. Unfortunately, due to time constraints, it was left in my desk drawer for a few years. After his death and my retirement, I finished the translation, although I wish I had completed it while he was alive.

*Release and repatriation

The favorable treatment of Flemish prisoners of war formed part of the Flamenpolitik (Flemish Policy). The policy had a racial foundation, since Nazi ideology argued that the Flemish were Germanic and therefore racially superior to the Walloons. It also hoped to encourage Flemish people to view Germany more favorably, paving the way for an intended annexation of the Greater Netherlands into the Greater Germanic Reich (Großgermanisches Reich). The Germans began actively repatriating Flemish prisoners of war in August 1940. By February 1941, 105,833 Flemish soldiers had been repatriated.[1]

See bibliography reference below

1]   Wikipedia contributors. (2019, September 16). Belgian prisoners of war in World War II. In Wikipedia, The Free Encyclopedia. Retrieved 14:27, April 3, 2020, from https://en.wikipedia.org/w/index.php?title=Belgian_prisoners_of_war_in_World_War_II&oldid=916086865